THE ORPHAN'S RESCUED NIECE

DOROTHY WELLINGS

CORNERSTONETALES.COM

1

BREAKING THE RULES

SOUTHWARK, LONDON, 1871

Beatrice Portly sat at the edge of the damp, mould-infested pavement waiting for her brother, Roy, who told her to not go anywhere otherwise he'd not be able to find her. Her brown shoes had thinned at the soles and water seeped between her toes as she kicked at the small puddles gathered in the potholes of Theed Street. She pulled her worn-out woollen coat to cover her nose. The smelly, unpleasant air was worse as the gutsy wind blew everything hither and thither in its path.

Oblivious to the wind, children from the neighbourhood laughed and kicked cans down the street, others built castles out of pebbles and rubble. Above the street, women were sharing stories as they hung wet clothes on ropes between the tenements. People had set up broken and chipped tables and chairs on the dire pavement in hopes of selling their wares.

Across the street, a middle-aged woman welcomed a man and a young boy covered in soot inside their house. She imagined it would be the same as their block. The five-story building with four tiny flats on each floor bulked with varied-sized families. She and Roy shared one room, Auntie Sadie slept on a cot in the corner of the living room cum kitchen, which had a table, three chairs and a cast iron stove with a grate.

"Hoi, why you sticking your feet in the water?"

Roy's croaky voice jammed in her ear as he sat beside her. His faded blue coat was thicker than when he'd left her earlier and his loosely-fitted cap was askew over his left ear.

"I'm bored. You were gone for hours," Beatrice said with a huff. "Next time I want to go with you."

"No, you can't."

"You always say that."

"It's 'cause you'll just get in the way."

"In the way of what?"

He grabbed her arm and pulled her to her feet. "Let's get home before Auntie Sadie does. She'll be in a dander if we're not there."

Beatrice side-glanced her brother with annoyance and noticed a shine inside his coat. She opened her mouth but knew better and said nothing. Roy grasped her hand and sprinted to the end of the street, squirming between narrow alleys until they crossed the Southwark Bridge over the dark, murky Thames River.

"Slow down," Beatrice said pulling her hand from her brother's grasp and said, "I can't run fast like you." She stopped and leaned over placing her palms over her knees, panting. Her mop hat fell to her soggy feet amidst the mushy ground and she seized it with a sigh. Aunt Sadie would reprimand her as she had cleaned it only yesterday.

"We're almost there, see?" Roy said, pointing to his left.

"Down Park Street, turn a few corners and then we're in Red Cross. It's not far."

"For you," said Beatrice between breaths, covering her head with the soiled hat. "Lant Street is far."

"Don't dally. Auntie Sadie is coming through Piccadilly so we don't have much time."

"I wanted to go to school," Beatrice said lifting her chin with a scowl on her face. "What do you think she's gonna say when I tell her I didn't go."

"Nothing, you say nothing, but a fine day."

Roy snapped her hand into his and dragged her behind him slipping past stationery wagons and with the slight of his hand grabbed whatever he could as they passed merchants. Those who saw him were too late and offered words of obscenity waving angry fists in the air.

"Take this," he said, shoving a hunk of dry bread into her hand as they snuck into an alleyway.

Beatrice's stomach growled. She hadn't eaten all day. Though she knew where he got the bread from, she took it and guilt filled her as she ate it.

"Now hurry, let's go," Roy urged, tugging on her arm. "Please, Bea, you know Auntie Sadie gets home early when she works in Piccadilly."

With a massive nod and not wanting to disappoint her brother, she said, "Yes, let's go, Roy."

She grabbed hold of his hand and they scurried through the streets and arrived home just as Auntie Sadie ambled around the corner, her large shoulder strap bag dangling from her shoulder.

"Put on the stove, quick!" Beatrice yelled, stomping up the whittled staircase behind her brother to the third floor. "I'll peel potatoes."

Behind one of the doors adjacent to them, a baby wailed.

The door rattled as Roy pushed the door open and he stumbled over the rutted floor. While Beatrice hurried to the tiny box in the corner of the larder where they kept a table, Roy grabbed the flint on the floor near the stove and within minutes a soft glow radiated from it.

Rubbing their hands they heard the door creak open followed by shuffling. Beatrice bolted to the table and picked up a knife, her heart thumped. Would Auntie Sadie know? Grown-ups had a way of knowing things. Her mind raced thinking of what to tell her aunt.

Auntie Sadie limped into the living room where Roy greeted her at the door, took the bag from her and placed it onto her cot.

"Did you have a good day?" Auntie Sadie said with a smile in her voice, sitting on a wobbly back-slated chair that Roy had placed near the grate for her.

"Oh yes," Roy answered with a bright grin.

"Must I chop the potatoes?" Beatrice said from the minuscule larder, and she saw her aunt nod through the gaps between the rotting timeworn boards of wood. Auntie's eyes were droopy and her face weary.

"Why don't you rest," Roy offered. "I'll get more water and help Bea cook supper."

"Helpful today, aren't you?" Auntie Sadie said with a raised brow. She kicked off her shoes and slid the chair forward toward the grate. "Makes me think you're up to no good again."

Roy's face drained of colour and his eyes widened in mock horror. "No, I'm gonna get more water and..." his voice dropped, but added a hint of cheer, "I got some vegetables and fruit. They aren't too fresh, but we can boil them."

Auntie Sadie's brows knitted. "You went to the market again, didn't you?"

When Roy remained silent and his eyes hit the floor, Auntie Sadie clicked her tongue with disdain.

"Why do you think I work extra days cleaning houses?" she said in a warbled voice. "To get us by, that's why. Do you want the bobbies to take you to the workhouse?"

Roy shook his head and stared at her, "No, I don't want that. I only want to help."

"I don't want Roy to go to the workhouse," Beatrice said, tears pricking her eyes. "We'll never see each other."

"Then go to school," Auntie Sadie peered at them both. "You didn't go to school, did you?" she glared at Beatrice, who shook her head.

"I'm sorry, I'll go tomorrow. I promise." Beatrice's heart thumped harder. "Please don't send Roy away, he's not thirteen yet, he can still come to school."

Auntie Sadie turned away and stared at the warm, flickering glow with a sigh. "I don't want either of you to go there. It's not good for families to be split up." Pointing at her bag she said, "Look inside. The Hembley's have thrown out clothes and shoes. There's an old dress and shoes for you, Beatrice, throw out the ones you have now. Trousers and a shirt for you, Roy."

Beatrice and Roy stared at each other in delight and whooped.

"Thank you, thank you," said Beatrice rushing towards their auntie's bag with Roy close behind her.

"Stop, Roy," Auntie Sadie said, glaring at him. "Fetch the water first. Think twice before leaving your sister alone and now I have to wash her hat again."

Roy's lips tipped downward and his head bobbed. "I'm sorry," he whispered and grabbed the pail before disappearing out the door.

Pain stabbed Beatrice's heart staring after him as she held onto the new dress, well, old, but it had no holes. She knew he meant well, but she wished her brother would listen. Roy, like many children, would steal and Auntie Sadie scolded him whenever she found out.

Beatrice pulled out two small black-heeled shoes. "Aunt Sadie, why do rich people throw out such nice things?" She inspected the shoes and decided they only needed a polish to shine.

Aunt Sadie rose to her feet. "Take off those shoes and dry your feet. You'll get sick. People get tired of the same clothes and want to look new and different."

"Would I look different in this new dress?" Beatrice said, holding up the dress to her shoulders, the hem stopped at her ankles.

Removing the grubby mop hat from Beatrice's head, Auntie Sadie planted a kiss on her head and said, "No, you're still pretty as you. You can't be anyone, but you. Go dry your feet and I'll take over supper."

Exaggerated *oofs* and *ah's* sounded from the door and Beatrice turned to her aunt giggling. She ran to the door and shifted it open for Roy staggering under the hefty weight of the pail, water spilling everywhere.

"Leave it by the door," Auntie Sadie said with a jerk of her head. "Try on the shirt and trousers, you're going to need them soon."

"What do you mean?" he said, digging inside her bag and pulling out brown trousers and a white cotton shirt with buttons.

"I'll tell you later," Auntie Sadie said.

"These are fancy, a bit big though. I'll grow into them, thank you."

Auntie Sadie walked to the pail of water and filled a pot to boil the potatoes. Turning to Roy she said, "Hand me those vegetables. You both look like waifs. We'll make do with the vegetables and have the fruit after supper."

Roy's face beamed and he dropped the clothes onto the cot. He dug into his coat and like a magician, he pulled out carrots and beans.

The Hembly's cook took a liking to Auntie Sadie and whenever there were leftovers, she shared them. Auntie Sadie had never looked happier announcing there'd be meat in the broth. She'd been given extra money and had bought fresh bread. Despite Auntie Sadie's disapproval, after supper, they'd enjoyed the apples and bananas Roy had provided.

With the candle burning on the stool in the living room, Beatrice loved hearing stories about the rich people and how they lived. Auntie Sadie told it like it was a fairytale. A house with rooms the size of their tenement and larger didn't sound real.

Auntie Sadie yawned and kissed them both on their cheeks. "I'll be going to sleep now. It's an early start to get to the Richardson House in Hyde Park. Don't stay up too late."

Once Auntie Sadie had gone to bed, Roy tapped Beatrice's hand and shoved something cool into her hand.

"Happy birthday," he said with a shy grin. "I'm sorry I couldn't get anything for you last week, but I couldn't find anything you'd like. You're nine now, practically a lady."

Beatrice's eyes widened with astonishment. Glancing from her brother to her hand, she was breathless. He'd given her a shiny brass bracelet in her hand with green, white, gold and pink beads.

"See, the green is like your eyes," his grin broadened, "the light pink is your hair. There are nine gold beads."

"Thank you," Beatrice stammered, choking over her words. It was the most beautiful thing she'd ever seen. "I love it, but-

but I can't keep this." She held it out to him. "Auntie Sadie would be angry if she knew."

His face turned solemn and he wrapped his hand over hers, pushing her hand back. "It's yours. You can't give away a present now, can you?"

"No, you're right," she said, shaking her head and tears gathered in her eyes. Leaning forward she embraced him. "I won't show Auntie Sadie. I'll keep it safe."

"Good," his bright grin returned. "Go sleep now. I need to meet up with some friends."

"But...it's night-time and—"

"Shush, Bea, you'll wake Auntie Sadie," he said covering her mouth with his forefinger. "I won't be late, promise. Go sleep now."

He hopped to his feet and gripped his coat, before hurrying out the door.

2
ETERNAL FRIENDSHIP

Roy stood tall on the pavement outside their house dressed in his well-fitted brown trousers and white button-up shirt. The night before Beatrice shined his shoes until she saw her reflection. The gloomy clouds could not hide his bright dimpled smile, the corners of his eyes creased as he stared at his sister.

"You look like a real young gentleman," Auntie Sadie said with pride in her voice. She stepped towards him and licked her thumb, brushing strands of his dark blonde hair from his face.

"Stop it, no need to fuss," Roy said turning his reddened face away, but his voice was full of excitement.

"Do you have to go?" Beatrice said, hands behind her back. She tried to be happy for her brother, but her heart was heavy. For as long as she remembered he'd been with her every day, the two of them, but it would be different now.

"Yeah, I have to go," Roy said in his croaky but deepened voice. He gazed down at her with a gleam in his eyes. In a matter of weeks, he'd grown taller than Auntie Sadie. "This is good. I can be somebody. Thanks to the real nice Sir in St. James where Auntie Sadie works, I will be an apprentice at the docks."

"Yeah, I know," Beatrice said biting on her lower lip. "It's not going to be the same anymore without you."

"Be brave," he said, placing a hand over her shoulder. "I'm gonna make money now, real good money and Auntie Sadie won't need to work so hard anymore. You understand, don't you?"

Beatrice averted her eyes to the dirt on the floor.

"Hoi, be brave, I know you can. I'll be home before dark every day. It's not like we're never gonna see each other."

"I'm going to miss you,"

"Bea, you'll be fine. Go to school and make friends. I'm sorry, maybe I stopped you from making friends around here, but all I wanted was to protect you."

"I know," Beatrice said, faking a smile when she saw worry cross his face. "You're right. I best learn to take care of myself and I'll make friends, I promise."

The grin returned to his face and he lifted his shoulders back. "Yes, of course you will. I'll be off now."

Making eye contact with her brother, Beatrice returned his joyous smile. She glanced at Auntie Sadie blowing kisses in the air and Roy's steps gradually skipped faster. Pursing her lips, Beatrice swiped the tears from her eyes before her aunt noticed.

"Come inside, dear," Auntie Sadie said. "Let's warm some of the fine tea Missus Hensley gifted to wish Roy some good luck. She was kind enough to give me the day off let's not waste it."

"Yes," said Beatrice staring down the street.

Auntie Sadie sighed and dug inside her pocket. "Here, take this coin and get something for Roy when he gets back."

Beatrice glimpsed at her aunt's outstretched hand and her eyes widened in awe. Her jaw slackened and said, "A shilling! Thank you. I can get Roy something great. I know what to get him."

"Hurry back now or your tea will get cold."

Grinning from ear to ear, Beatrice swirled on her heels and ran down the street with her aunt's words of caution sailing past her ears. Scuttling past people and racing against the wagons and carriages she decided she could beat a horse.

The market wasn't busy and she gazed between shops until she found a toy shop. Roy had outgrown most of his toys, but he loved his collection of spinning tops. The toy shop sold carved wooden painted ones and she chose one with horizontal blue and white stripes. If there was enough money left over, she'd buy him a bag of sweets.

Satisfied with her choice, she paid the shopkeeper, who had thick white whiskers and hairy eyes peering at her as she gave him the money. She thanked him and capered out of the shop. Oblivious to her surroundings, Beatrice toppled against a girl about her age.

"Oof, that hurt," the girl with dark curly hair said rubbing her behind on the pavement.

Flushed, Beatrice's hand flew to her mouth. "I'm sorry, I didn't see you..." she held out her hand, "Let me help you up."

"Thank you," the girl said, soaring over Beatrice's head. "It's alright, I wasn't watching where I was going. I do that a lot, I think, that's what my father says, '*Tilly, look before you walk*' all the time," she said deepening her voice with a chuckle, lifting her arm into the air.

"You're funny," Beatrice said laughing at the girl's poor imitation of her father. "Is your name Tilly?"

"Uh-huh," Tilly nodded. "Tilly Kent. It's nice to meet you."

"Yes, you, too. I'm Beatrice Portly, but my brother and... well, if I had friends they'd call me Bea, too."

"Can I call you, Bea?"

"You'll be my friend?" Beatrice said skirting past the toy shop door as someone pushed past the girls.

"I'd love to be your friend. Let me ask my father or maybe you can ask him and I can come over to your house to play."

"Where do you live?"

"In White Street, it's not far from here."

"I know that street, it crosses over and two streets away from me. I'm in Lant Street."

"Yes, let's go. What did you buy from the toy shop?" Tilly said, peering at the brown bag in Beatrice's hands.

Walking side by side, Beatrice explained how her brother started working at the docks and she'd bought a gift for him.

"Your brother's lucky to have a sister like you," Tilly babbled with an upbeat smile.

"Do you have a brother?"

"No, it's just me and my Dad. I had a baby sister. She died with my mum when she was born. Her name was Betty. I don't remember them because Dad says I was two years old. I would have loved a sister."

"I'm sorry. I never knew my parents. They died soon after I was born. There was a breakout of cholera. Roy and I live with Auntie Sadie. She's kind and takes care of us."

"I know!" Tilly blurted with gusto. She stopped and grabbed Beatrice's arms. Her eyes shimmered with enthusiasm. "We could be sisters, can't we?"

"Okay, yes, I've always wanted a sister. Then you'd have a brother, too." Beatrice felt her heart would explode with joy. Roy would be pleased she'd made a friend, not just any friend, but a sister. "My Auntie Sadie will like you a lot."

"What a beautiful bracelet," said Tilly, her eyes admiring

the gift Roy had given Beatrice for her birthday. The bracelet had slid to her wrist peeking from beneath the edge of her coat. Beatrice had worn it enough times for Auntie Sadie to pretend not to notice it and she never took it off her arm.

"It was a birthday gift from my brother. I can't wait to give him this present. He'll be home later, maybe you'll meet him."

Tilly lived in a tiny house with two rooms and a living room that expanded into a kitchen. Beatrice stared in awe at the small unkempt weed-infested garden where Mr Kent was building and repairing wooden chairs. He had curly hair like Tilly and Beatrice noticed his snug clothes stretching at the seams. His moustache curled at the ends and his shaggy beard hung below his chin.

"Be back before dark," Mr Kent said with a smile and returned to his work adding, "Have fun with your new friend."

"I will," Tilly yelled over her shoulder as she scampered down the street with Beatrice at her side.

"What would you like to do?" Beatrice said, ambling up the stairs to the third floor of their tenement. "I've got sticks and straw. We could make dolls."

"We could make each other dolls and play hopscotch. I've wanted to play that game for a long time, but no one wanted to play with me. They all said they were busy."

Beatrice nodded, "I love that game, too, but I haven't been to school in a while, because I need to help my Auntie Sadie. She hasn't been well these past few days, but she has medicine and says she's feeling better."

Beatrice pushed the door open with her shoulder, and holding the brown bag in her arms said, "I'm back and got something real nice for Roy. I made a new friend, Tilly. Can we play outside?"

"A new friend?" Auntie Sadie said lifting her head. She was

on her knees leaning over a wooden barrel washing clothes and a curious smile stretched on her face.

"Hello, ma'am," Tilly said with a polite smile. "Please can I play with Bea? We met outside the toy shop. My dad says it's alright. I only need to be home 'fore dark."

"You're a darling, pumpkin. Go on, it's fine. Enjoy yourselves." Auntie Sadie said, giving Beatrice a quick wink, chuckling as she continued washing the clothes.

Beatrice placed the gift for Roy on the table, grasped Tilly's hand and they bounded downstairs.

"I changed my mind," Beatrice said grinning at the confused expression on Tilly's face. "Let's play hopscotch. The dolls will take too long to make."

"Yes," Tilly agreed.

They gathered small pebbles and created a series of small squares on the pavement.

Beatrice was thrilled and imagined how happy Roy would be knowing she'd made a friend. She lost track of time as they each had a few turns jumping between the squares,

"That looks fun, can I have a turn?"

Beatrice's heart soared like the wind whooshing leaves into the sky. Roy's bag slung over his shoulder and his face full of fatigue stared at her with his mischievous lop-sided grin.

"Roy!" Beatrice raced to him and wrapped her arms around him. "I missed you. I went to the shop and got you something. I did what you said and I made a friend."

Glancing from Beatrice to Tilly, he breathed a sound she'd never heard from him. Beatrice lifted her chin and frowned. His eyes were wide, cheeks flushed and his lips parted, but he remained silent.

"Roy?" Beatrice tugged on his arm harder.

"Yes? Bea, yes, what is it?" he said, glancing between his sister and Tilly. "Who is she?" he turned to gaze at Beatrice.

"My new friend, Tilly," Beatrice said, taking a step backwards and staring at her brother with a frown and a lump formed at the back of her throat. What was wrong with Roy? She turned to Tilly with a shake of her head. "Excuse my brother, he's acting strange. Let's go—" Beatrice glimpsed at her new friend, eyes wide open. Tilly's cheeks were red and her head tilted as she returned Roy's stare, her eyes continually looking away, but returning to him.

Beatrice didn't know why, but she didn't like this reaction. Her heart palpitated and her eyes dampened. What did this mean? Tilly had lost interest in their game and started to talk to Roy, whose face shone like the star on a Christmas tree.

3
UNEXPECTED CHANGES

NINE YEARS LATER, 1880

Beatrice's joints and muscles ached with every step. As much as she loved Roy, she hoped he wouldn't be home yet. Since the day he and Tilly met, they were inseparable. Though a childish thought, she wished they'd never met. On that day she lost her brother and the first friend she'd ever made.

Adjusting the strap over her shoulder, Beatrice reminisced about the day she first started cleaning wealthy people's houses by herself. At fourteen years old, Auntie Sadie took her to the houses where she cleaned and taught Beatrice everything she knew. A few days later, Auntie Sadie started with a cough and a light fever forcing her to stay in bed.

Auntie Sadie had good and bad days but didn't return to work again as her sickness took control over her body. When Beatrice had arrived home after cleaning the house in Picadilly, she expected to find Roy home taking care of Auntie Sadie, instead, she found him and Tilly seated at the table with a bottle of alcohol. The strong, malty odour drained all oxygen in the tiny flat. Leaving the door open, she hurried to open the top window in the living room, suctioning out the stuffy air. Auntie Sadie was, fortunately, fast asleep and was not disturbed by the noise from the table.

"Roy? Tilly?" Beatrice had frowned at them. Both laughed and with hazy eyes appeared happy to see her.

"Thit... sit... down," Roy had slurred and Tilly giggled. "H... have some." He reached for the bottle, his fingers stumbling around it.

"No, I don't want any," Beatrice's heart flooded with sadness. Her body burned with fatigue and her stomach growled. "Where'd you get this?"

"My dad," said Tilly, her head lolling from side to side. "He washn't home... I got it..." her voice trailed and she chortled. "He'll nev...er know, 'cause he's... a drunk."

"You're supposed to be looking after Auntie Sadie," Beatrice said, her fingers rolling into her hands, glaring at her brother. "She's not well."

"Sleeping, sleeping," Roy answered the words loose on his tongue. "All day now."

"Please, Bea, have some," Tilly begged and grabbed the bottle holding it up to her. "It's great."

Against her better judgment and to stop the consistent nagging, she relented and took the bottle. Roy clapped his hands in delight and Tilly's eyes sparkled with satisfaction and joy.

Placing the bottle to her lips, Beatrice took a swig and almost fainting, spat it out spluttering and slammed the bottle onto the table.

"That's disgusting! How can you drink that? You're going to land yourselves in trouble."

"Don't kick... up a shine, nothing's wrong," his deep croaky voice was muffled in her ears.

"I'm going to bed," Beatrice stated and left the two at the table, putting her bag on the floor. Adding more coal to the stove, she stoked up the low glow of the fire before lying beside Auntie Sadie. Her aunt needed warmth. Heartbroken, she bit on her lower lip to suppress her tears missing her kind brother and loyal friend.

Beatrice slipped out of her daze as she was about to step across the road. A carriage raced past her, the driver screaming and pointing a crooked finger at her. From head to toe, she was covered in dirt and wet sludge from the carriage wheels slicing through the filmy puddles gathered inside various-sized ruts along the street. She stopped at the side of the pavement and breathed a sigh of misery.

Every night she dreamt that it was only a horrible dream and that it was a phase Tilly and Roy were going through. She'd thought one of them would break the other's heart and had decided to be a good friend and sister, but that day never happened. As time passed, the relationship deepened and became thicker than Auntie Sadie's potato broth.

She and Tilly barely spoke and she remembered them as young children promising to be sisters. Never did Beatrice imagine that her brother would become infatuated with the first friend she'd ever made.

Now that Roy was a full-time worker at the docks and got home at different hours, she had no idea what to expect. Some days Roy would come home at late hours after visiting Tilly or he'd bring Tilly to their home. Auntie Sadie didn't approve, but she didn't discourage the relationship either. Beatrice guessed that her aunt was too weak and sick to challenge her brother.

Bowing her head, she rushed down Friar Street as fast as her weary legs could carry her and turned into Lant Street. A nauseating plethora of smells wafting through the air from the tenements as people began cooking, uniting with the rot from the Thames River engulfed her nose and resting on her tongue. Coughing and gagging, she covered her nose with her coat and gazed down the street thankful to be a few houses away from home. Despite the cold foul air children, dressed in rags, ran about splashing in the silvery-green puddles and screamed in delight.

She walked inside and climbed the narrow stairs as if they were steep mountains. The house on Picadilly was beautiful and she enjoyed cleaning it, but it was huge and took time. Fortunately, the mistress had employed other cleaners to focus on different areas of the house. With a grunt, she forced the front door open and welcomed the silence. Roy must be visiting Tilly and Auntie Sadie had been feeling better. Beatrice guessed her aunt may have gone for a short walk.

Closing the door, her thoughts were interrupted by her aunt's rattling cough. Surprised, Beatrice strode into the room and stopped, agape, staring at her aunt, brother and Tilly seated at the table. Their faces were forlorn, but the blatant guilt over Roy and Tilly's faces gave her the impression they'd done something or were to tell her bad news. Both avoided eye contact, Roy rubbed his hand behind his neck and Tilly shifted in her seat.

"What's going on?" Beatrice said with apprehension in her voice. When it came to Roy and Tilly it was never a surprise, only complications. She lost count of how much money Roy had borrowed from her, despite him earning more.

"Please sit," Auntie Sadie said in a weathered voice, a troubled look washed over her face and her eyes were full of disappointment.

"What is it?" Beatrice asked again, obeying her aunt and sat on a chair between her aunt and Tilly.

Roy and Tilly exchanged the same expression of guilt and remorse before gazing at her.

"I... I don't know how to tell you this, Bea," Tilly started and the words choked in her throat.

Beatrice cringed at the sound of her nickname from Tilly's sweet voice and noticed Roy clutching her hand.

"What Tilly, and me, need to tell you is," Roy drew in a sharp breath, "Tilly is going to have a baby, my baby." He forced a smile. "Isn't that good news, right?"

Auntie Sadie looked away with a click of her tongue.

The air rushed at Beatrice's skin, engulfing her as if being sucked into a black hole, and she blinked. Speechless, she glanced at her aunt, who inclined her head with furrowed brows.

"I've agreed that Tilly can move in with us," Auntie Sadie said. Her warbled, but stern voice indicated her decision was made. "There will be a small, discreet wedding. I'll speak to the local church."

"What about Mr Kent?" Beatrice blurted in horror. "Does he not have a say? Does he know?"

Tilly hung her head in shame and nodded as tears rolled down her cheeks. "Yes, he does and wants no part in the baby's life. I am dead to him," she said in a soft tone, sniffling.

Sympathy tugged at Beatrice's heart watching her friend break down in tears. She hadn't seen Mr Kent in years and found it hard to believe he'd turn his back on Tilly, but she and her brother were a bewildering pair.

"I'm sorry," Beatrice said sitting closer to Tilly. "I'm sure he'll come around. He'll want to know his grandchild."

"No," Tilly said wiping her eyes. "He's changed over the years. I think he forgot about me years ago. If not for Roy," she turned to him with a smile, "I'd never have made it through the tough times with my father."

"I'm gonna pull in extra hours and make more money for the baby. My friend at the docks will help out with a crib. He said it's old and needs repairs, but that's fine. I'm happy, Bea. Imagine me... a father." His face beamed with a perky smile as if the realisation had dawned on him.

"I... I don't know what to say," Beatrice said, overwhelmed and astounded at the news. She was to become an aunt like Auntie Sadie was to them. "This is big. When people find out—"

"After the wedding," Auntie Sadie said, lifting her chin. "Until then, no one is to breathe a word."

Beatrice offered a smile to her brother and Tilly, "I suppose we will be sisters now and I'm happy for you. I can't imagine becoming an aunt, but..." she glimpsed at Auntie Sadie, "I'll be a good one."

THE PARISH AT ST. John Horsleydown church in Fair Street was pleased that Tilly and Roy wanted to join in holy matrimony and accommodated Auntie Sadie's request. She hadn't wanted to lie to the parish and explained the situation.

Beatrice loved the symmetrical stone-faced building, it had an aisled nave and jutting spire that touched the clouds in the shape of a tapering column with a weather vane at the top. Although the church had a peal of ten bells, they did not ring.

The sun shone brightly through the large Venetian window in the centre as if blessing the ceremony. And the joyous occasion was contagious as Roy and Tilly were overjoyed, exchanging their vows; and Auntie Sadie shed tears. Though Beatrice was thrilled for the newlyweds, her mind pricked at the responsibility of taking care of a baby. Could the happy couple do it? Would they be able to give up their life of freedom and give their utmost attention and love to their child?

Since Roy had discovered he was to become a father, he worked harder and saved money instead of spending it. Beatrice watched Tilly's belly grow and affection grew in her heart. A tiny life was growing inside her sister, her brother's child.

Beatrice had moved out of the room she'd shared with Roy. She felt better sleeping by her aunt's side and caring for her. Although Tilly hadn't brought much when she moved in, the flat was cramped. Whenever Beatrice could, she helped Auntie Sadie take short walks on her good days as the illness grew worse.

A nurse from the local community came to visit and treat Auntie Sadie and would examine Tilly's progress and excitement grew as the time for the baby's birth approached. Beatrice requested time off from the houses she cleaned and didn't mind that she'd lose pay. Her aunt and the baby's birth were more important.

"I worry, Bea," said Auntie Sadie in a weary tone. "I desire to see the baby, but I fear at my dizzying age my time is near."

"Don't talk that way," Beatrice said, handing her a warm cup of tea. "Here drink this, you'll feel better. Later, I'll give you the medicine Nurse Helen left for you."

"Thank you, dear," Auntie Sadie said, accepting Beatrice's help to sit up in the cot. As she drank her tea, Beatrice tucked blankets around her aunt.

"How exciting to think that the baby will come anytime now," Beatrice said, shooting a smile in her aunt's direction. "Roy has been great, hasn't he? The baby has been good for him."

"Yes, a baby brings much change. He or she will need a lot of love, care and attention." Auntie Sadie blew into her cup and took a sip. "Tilly will be a good mother. I've seen the way she talks to the child."

"Do you think the baby hears her?"

Auntie Sadie answered with a confident smile. "Yes, I think so. Your mother spoke to you and Roy when she was pregnant and when you both were born," she smiled, "it was as though you both knew everything already."

"Amazing," Beatrice said, sitting at the edge of the bedside. "Maybe—"

A groan of pain resonated throughout the tiny flat and Beatrice exchanged an expression of worry with her aunt.

"Go," Auntie Sadie said, gesticulating in the air. Another shrill of pain. "I think the baby is coming. Roy will be home soon and you should call the nurse. I'll do my best to help Tilly."

"Alright," Beatrice said, her heart thumping. Was the baby coming? She rushed to Tilly's side, she lay on the bed holding her stomach and writhing in pain. "Hold on, I'm going to get the nurse."

Tilly gritted her teeth as she nodded.

By the time Beatrice arrived with the nurse, Roy was home and with Auntie Sadie's guidance had gathered towels and a bucket of warm water.

"Clear out," Nurse Helen instructed and chased Roy out of the room. "But not you," she said, pointing at Beatrice. "I will need your help."

Hours passed by until Tilly's cries grew louder and faster.

"What's happening?" Roy shouted into the room.

"The baby's coming," Beatrice exhaled with excitement. "Tell Auntie Sadie, she'll meet the baby."

Beatrice handed the nurse more warm, damp towels and replaced them as directed.

"One more time, push," Nurse Helen said and Tilly screamed.

Within minutes, the sound of a baby's wails echoed throughout the flat, followed by shouts of joy.

"It's a girl," Beatrice yelled watching the nurse wrap and place the baby into Tilly's arms. Beatrice noticed the sweat glimmering off Tilly's body and with a cool, damp cloth wiped her beaming face.

Nurse Helen pulled the curtain back and called in Roy who bolted inside and stood beside his wife, cooing at the baby. Beatrice watched Roy take the baby girl into his arms and tears filled his eyes.

"I'm a father," he said to Beatrice with a giant grin.

With a nod from Tilly, Roy left the room and walked toward Auntie Sadie.

Roy sat on the bed and Auntie Sadie's face lit up.

"Auntie Sadie, meet your great-niece. Her name is Sadie." His grin extended to his sparkling green eyes.

With a joyous smile, Auntie Sadie stuck out her pinkie finger and the baby clutched it with its tiny hand.

"Thank you, Roy, be a good father," she said with tears in her eyes and he nodded with a bright grin. Glancing at Beatrice with love etched on her face she said, "I loved you both as my own and now you must do the same."

"I will," Beatrice insisted, her heart leaped gazing at the tiny bundle in Roy's arms.

She turned to her aunt and froze, tears welling in her eyes. Beatrice dropped to her knees and grasped her aunt's hand. Peace had fallen upon Auntie Sadie's face, closing her eyes, her head lolled to one side as she took her last breath.

4
TWIST OF PROVIDENCE

Five years had gone by since Auntie Sadie passed away and there was not a day Beatrice didn't miss her. She knew her aunt would have loved to watch baby Sadie grow into the beautiful energetic girl that she'd become with a mind that carried a vivid imagination and full of curiosity.

Beatrice hung up the last of the damp clothes inside the house and turned to Tilly, who was mending a dress for Sadie.

"How did Sadie enjoy her first day at school?" Beatrice asked. "She was sleeping when I got home."

"Loved it," Tilly said with a small smile. "She told me about the children and she likes her teacher, who is teaching them letters. In no time, she'll be able to write her name. I'm sure she'll tell you all about it when you return."

"If she's awake," Beatrice responded with a chuckle. "I may be back late. A new family has moved into a house in Kennington Lane, near the park. I'll be heading there and imagine the place must be quite a mess. The house has been empty for a few months."

Beatrice dragged the door open and returned Tilly's smile,

waving goodbye. The door banged shut and Beatrice hopped down the stairs remembering her days in school; the enormous room crawling with children of all ages, long benches and tables.

Despite Roy working hard at the docks and earning a promotion, Beatrice worked longer hours to help bring in extra money.

Kennington was not far from Southwark and Beatrice was thrilled to be appointed to be hired as the cleaner. Whenever she walked past the boarded house, she'd thought its overgrown fauna would be stunning with the touch of a gardener. The windows had been thick with dust and dirt had gathered amidst the peeling paint. It was a shame to see the abandoned house deteriorate.

Beatrice gaped at the house. The repainted black cast iron gate opened with a gentle push. She noticed the front garden had been sheared with low neatly trimmed bushes following thick stones that bordered the walkway and admired the angelic statue placed at the corner edge of the bordered walkway. Small trees and bushes had been cut back revealing the balconies on the first floor.

She walked up the stairs passing two columns that supported a portico to the front door and lifted the door knocker allowing it to clap against the impressive painted black wooden door.

The door opened and a man dressed in a neat black and white uniform greeted her with a bright smile.

"Talloway Residence, how can I help you?" he gave a quizzical stare, eyeing her from head to toe.

"Hello, I'm Beatrice Portly, and—"

"Ah, the cleaner," he said, slapping his hands together as if sense had returned to him and she guessed he'd been confused. Who'd consider a meeting with her? In comparison to the clothes worn by the wealthy, she stuck out like a pigeon amongst peacocks.

"Welcome, I'm Mr Burkes, the butler." He gesticulated for her to enter. "We've been expecting you. At the end of the passage," he said beckoning her to follow him, "is where you'll find all you need and the changing room. You'll be expected to wear the uniform provided."

She offered a thankful smile as he chattered away explaining the rooms leading her towards the room which she knew would be more of a cleaning closet. The floors shone and she noticed the Renaissance paintings and other artworks that she was unfamiliar with hanging from the walls. It was nothing she'd imagined it to be. The interior was magnificent and grander than it appeared from the outside.

"The bedrooms are on the first floor and if you need assistance or encounter a problem, please come to me immediately," he said as they arrived outside the utility room. "One other thing, you are not to speak to anyone. Although the Talloways are mostly out during the day, Miss Felicia and her governess, Miss Parker spends the days in her sleeping quarters. They may tour the garden or go on excursions at times."

"That sounds exciting," Beatrice said. "And thank you, I'm sure I'll manage."

With a satisfied expression on his narrow face, he left her standing at the end of the passage.

Holding her breath, she exhaled and opened the door. Expecting a tiny room with shelves leaving barely enough space for the cleaning equipment, she was astonished to discover it was one of the largest utility rooms she'd ever had to work with. There was space for her to get changed into her uniform and beneath one of the shelves was a place where she could comfortably place her bag.

Despite the black uniform being a size too large, it was

comfortable and the extra folds were hidden by the white pinafore. Gathering the cleaning materials and equipment she required, Beatrice set off to start cleaning the parlour.

The beige drapes were open and sunlight shone through two adjacent Victorian windows with its two grid panel design. The room was swept with a variety of lavish furniture and a fireplace with a mantel held what appeared to be family photographs. Gold, red, and tan coloured upholstered couches surrounded a mahogany rectangular table where a man sat on a couch reading a book. He looked up as Beatrice entered and she blushed.

He appeared to be around her age, had a prominent square jaw, eyes the colour of hazelnuts and dark wavy hair curled from his ears to the top of his head.

"Oh, I'm sorry. I didn't know anyone was in here."

He snapped the book shut and turned his body positioning to face her, his face full of amusement.

"Where do you think I should go?"

Her cheeks flushed and her heart pounded in her ears. Had she offended him? Mr Burkes did say to not speak to anyone.

"Uh, no, sorry, that is not what I meant. You see I'm the new cleaner and I, well—"

A grin filled his clean-shaven masculine face and he laughed as though his belly would explode.

"No, forgive me, I'm teasing," he said, spluttering as his joyous laughter came to an end. "I didn't mean to scare you. My name is Oscar Talloway. I'm hiding away from my father. He's expecting me to meet him with business associates, but I suspect he has other intentions in which I'm not interested."

"I see," Beatrice said, exhaling a soft sigh of relief. "Won't he be angry?"

Oscar shrugged. "Perhaps, but I will deal with it later." He held up his book. "I prefer reading to entertaining people I don't know."

"I like reading, too," Beatrice said, digging for her cleaning materials. If Mr Burkes caught her talking to Mr Talloway and not working, he may become angry.

"Where are you from?"

"Southwark," Beatrice said, avoiding eye contact, and began to clean the fireplace.

"Do you enjoy cleaning houses?"

She glimpsed at him with a frown. Who would enjoy cleaning houses?

"I don't mind besides it's a means to earn money. I don't know if people enjoy their jobs, but my brother does."

"You have a brother? Where does he work?"

"At the docks. He had a promotion and maybe in a few months we'll move into a bigger home."

"You live with your brother?"

Beatrice nodded and said with a fond smile, "He married my best friend and they have a beautiful little girl. She's five years old. Named after my deceased Auntie Sadie."

She was relieved to have her back to him on her knees polishing the grate and wiping her eyes with the back of her hand. It was hard to talk about Auntie Sadie.

"Oh, I'm sorry to hear about your aunt," his voice was croaky.

Beatrice assumed he'd resumed reading and stood to her feet to sweep up the remnants of the soot and ash. She turned and found him staring at her.

"Can I get you something?" Beatrice said and swallowed, returning his intense stare.

"I'd like to talk more, but I need to leave." He appeared disappointed. "As it turns out, I do need to meet with my father and I was stalling for time," he flashed a charming smile.

"Next time you come I'll make sure the house is extra untidy and you'll have to stay longer."

Beatrice giggled and pushed a strand of hair behind her ear.

"There'll be soot all over the room and mountains of food everywhere," he said with an enormous grin, holding his book beneath his armpit. "It was good to meet you, Beatrice, I'm sure I'll see you again."

"Yes, and you, Mr Talloway."

"No, Oscar, please," he said shaking his head. "No formalities. That is if you don't mind me calling you by your first name. My apologies, I didn't ask you first." His cheeks turned crimson.

"It's alright, Mr Tallo—uh, Oscar. You can call me by my first name."

He lifted his chin and appeared delighted. "Very well, good day, and happy cleaning," he said with a wink and Beatrice returned a smile watching him leave.

Humming as she finished the parlour and found cleaning the other rooms easier and quicker than ever before. She couldn't stop thinking about her brief encounter with Oscar and smiled. He was an unusual man.

Beatrice was exhausted as she left the Talloway house, pleased that Mr Burkes wanted her to return three times the following week. She hoped Tilly would cook her infamous tasty potato and meat soup.

She climbed the steps and found the front door ajar. Frowning, Beatrice opened the door and found Sadie with a tear-stained face bending over Tilly, who was lying on the floor, holding a wet cloth to her mother's forehead.

5
TRAGEDY STRIKES

When Beatrice arrived home Roy was sitting near the cast iron stove stoking the fire and tiny Sadie sat beside her mother feeding her broth. Beatrice sat beside her brother and placed her hand over his and noticed his damp eyes. If he added any more coals the fire would burn out.

"Another spoon, Mama," said Sadie in her soft, peaceful voice.

"Thank you, sweetie," Tilly answered in a weak voice.

Beatrice smiled at the beautiful, but heart-wrenching scene of a five-year-old taking care of her sickly mother.

"You can leave the fire, it won't burn out," Beatrice said.

With a sigh, Roy dropped the stoker near the stove.

"Don't worry, the church is praying Roy and I'm sure the medicine will work," Beatrice said with hope in her heart, trusting her encouragement would reach him.

Roy pulled his hand away and anger flashed in his eyes, his chest heaving. "Yeah? Then why isn't it working already? It's been two months and she's getting no better."

"He's given new medicine. The doctor knows what he's doing."

"Well, we will see about that. We're poor, he's given us stuff the rich people don't want."

"Daddy?" a tiny voice rang and Roy exchanged a worried glance with Beatrice. "Mama will get better, won't she?"

"Yes," Beatrice offered a reassuring smile to the girl's furrowed face. Sadie held the spoon in mid-air. "The doctor has given her new medicine."

Beatrice nudged her brother and whispered, "Tell her!"

"Sadie," Roy glimpsed at her but avoided eye contact. "Aunt Bea is right. The doctor that came brought new medicine. He said Mama will feel better in a few days. First, her fever will go away. Her coughing will take a bit longer, she needs fresh air."

Her dimpled smile reached her sparkling green eyes. Without another word, she continued to feed her mother. Beatrice heard Sadie's whispers of hope spoken to her mother.

"It's a lie," Roy said, lowering his voice and attempting to calm down. "You shouldn't give her false hope."

Indignation filled Beatrice's belly and she drew in a deep breath, releasing it she said, "I can't believe that Tilly won't recover."

"Mama's finished eating," said Sadie with a gigantic yawn. "I think she wants to sleep now."

"Alright, you best go to bed, too," Roy said climbing to his feet. "Say goodnight to Mama."

Tears filled Sadie's eyes and she nodded. Leaning over her mother, Sadie kissed her cheek and said, "Goodnight, Mama. I'll help you eat in the morning."

"Mm... I love you, Sadie," Tilly said, her voice barely audible in the minuscule flat.

Sadie dawdled from her mother's side towards her cot

placed near the stove. Her face was downcast. Even in the dark with flickering shadows across the walls, Beatrice noticed Sadie's eyes were misty.

Beatrice rose to her feet and stood beside her niece, "You're a brave girl. Your dad and I are proud of you." Beatrice said and gave Sadie a tight squeeze. "There's no need to cry, your mama is doing her best to fight this illness."

Hacking and coughing sounded from the room where Tilly was sleeping and Roy jumped to his feet to tend to his wife.

"Mama is very sick. Will she really get better?" Sadie's voice warbled as she wiped tears from her cheeks.

"Your dad called in another doctor and he has given new medicine. He says it will work," Beatrice said offering a reassuring smile. "Do you want me to tell you a story?"

"Yes," Sadie's curls bounced around her head.

"I know your mama would love to and when she's better she can tell you stories again," Beatrice said, helping her into her bed. "I will tell you the story of the tortoise and the hare. Would you like that?"

Sadie nodded and lay down on the cot, yawning. Beatrice stroked her dark curls and told her about the race between the tortoise and the hare. Halfway through the story, Sadie was fast asleep her chest rising and falling as she drew in deep, soothing breaths.

Beatrice covered Sadie with an extra blanket and searched for Roy, who was seated beside Tilly's sleeping form, holding her hand.

"It's like Auntie Sadie all over again," Roy said, his voice broken and shaky. "What'll I do if I lose her, Bea?" he stared at Beatrice as if she had all the answers.

Holding her breath, she swallowed and exhaled staggered breath. "It won't. We need to believe that the medicine will work."

"She's been this way for a long time. She's getting worse. I didn't want to admit it or think it, but she is."

"Think of Sadie, you need to be strong for her," Beatrice said in a whisper.

"I took some days off to help her," Roy said, raking his hand through his dishevelled hair. His eyelids drooped and Beatrice noticed the exhaustion on his face.

"Would you like tea?"

He shook his head staring at Tilly.

Beatrice's heart tugged with pain noticing the worry etched on his face. She worried about her best friend. As much as she tried and wanted to believe in Tilly's recovery, she had doubts. Would they see Tilly's bright smile again or her confident laugh? She had to be strong for Roy and Sadie.

"Why don't you get some sleep, I'll tend to Tilly for a few hours. We can take turns."

He stared at her with an anxious frown. "How can I sleep?"

"You must otherwise you can't help her. I can see you're exhausted. I'll watch over her. If there's a problem I'll wake you, I promise."

Roy glanced between his wife and Beatrice and finally relented. Wiping his eyes, he lay down beside Tilly, pulling a blanket over his body and within seconds he was snoring away.

The days turned into weeks and Roy spent more money on medicine, but nothing worked. Tilly had good days where she could get out of bed, but other days she was too weak to lift a finger. Roy would sing their favourite songs to her in his croaky, tuneless voice and Sadie would join in, seated in her father's lap.

Another month passed by and Tilly's fevers grew worse and she appeared to become weaker, unable to cough. Her face was gaunt and pallid and her body was skin and bone. Beatrice would never forget the first day of the fourth month, waking up to Roy's screams and wails. She jumped out of bed telling Sadie to wait, but she didn't listen. They raced towards the little room, Beatrice had shared with Roy as children and found him holding Tilly, limp, in his arms.

∽

LIFE AT HOME had not been the same since Tilly died. A cloud of depression had settled over her usually cheerful brother and Sadie became withdrawn. Beatrice's heart tugged with sorrow the more she thought of the events since Tilly became sick. None of the doctors knew what had caused it. At first, it was a chest infection and then it became something else. Aside from the pain that gripped her heart at the absence of her friend, she couldn't imagine what Roy and Sadie were feeling. She knew Roy had loved Tilly more than life itself.

She arrived early at the Talloway house and greeted Mr Burke as she usually did, attempting a smile that did not reach her eyes. As she walked down the passage, she felt his eyes bore into the back of her head and guessed he must've noticed a change in her.

"Beatrice, how are you? It's been a while, hasn't it?" Oscar's cheery voice said as he strode down the passage.

She frowned. Drowning in her thoughts, she hadn't noticed him walk down the lush carpeted staircase.

"Hello, Oscar," was all Beatrice could muster. She couldn't offer even a smile.

"What's wrong?" His brows knitted and his bright smile faded. "Has something happened? I've never seen you this way."

Uncontrollable tears formed in Beatrice's eyes and she

tried to avoid eye contact, but with his forefinger, he lifted her chin.

"Let's talk in the parlour. I'll get Mr Burke to arrange tea. It looks like you need some care."

"No, I need... to work," she stammered, choking over her words, clutching the cleaning equipment tight.

"I insist, go inside, please." His tone was unchanging and she realised he wouldn't take *no* for an answer.

He disappeared and after a few minutes, he returned and instructed her to sit on the couch.

Oscar pulled out a handkerchief and offered it to her. "You need this more than I do."

"Oh, I couln't—" she sniffled.

"Take it. I have more where that came from."

He sat beside her and said in a comforting tone, "You can trust me. I won't tell anyone. Please, tell me what's troubling you."

A male servant entered the parlour and placed a tray with two china cups of tea on the table and Oscar thanked him.

Wiping her eyes, cheeks and nose, Beatrice exhaled sharp breaths and hesitated before telling him about Tilly, her sickness and passing away, her brother and Sadie.

"It's affected my brother in a way I never thought. He's depressed and has gone back to drinking again. Sadie is hurting and needs him, but I can't get through to him. He only sees his grief." She hiccupped and drew in a breath. "I hope it doesn't affect his work. He's been doing well and I hope he won't fall back and become a drunkard like he was before Sadie was born."

"I'm sorry to hear that, it's terrible, a tragedy. I-I can't imagine your pain."

Beatrice glanced at him and appreciated the concern on his face and his kind, sympathetic words of encouragement.

"What's worse," Beatrice gasped, "Is that Sadie's alone at home... alone. There is no one to take her to school and collect her. While I make sure she has something to eat, I worry about her. The neighbours check on her, but they get busy and also work."

"What? How old is she?" said Oscar in horror.

"She's five years old." A small, proud smile touched her lips. "She's a good girl, and..."

"You come here three times a week, don't you?" he said in a stern tone.

Beatrice stared at him in surprise at the unexpected question and nodded. She gazed into his intense dark eyes filled with determination and tenacity.

"Bring her here with you, I insist. A little girl who's lost her mother can't sit at home with no one to support her." He shook his head and his face was full of compassion.

"Oh, I couldn't impose on you like that," Beatrice said, her heart thumped and the air was suffocating. She'd love to bring Sadie, but what would Roy say? Despite the offers from neighbours, Roy had instructed Sadie to stay home and not to go to school.

"It's fine, I'll arrange a guest room for her. My sister has some old toys your niece can play with."

"Are you sure?" Beatrice's cheeks were hot. She'd need to speak to Roy, but if Sadie was with her it would ensure her niece's safety.

"I insist, please, don't make me say it again. Next time you come here and every day going forward when you work here, I expect to see the little girl. She can help you if she doesn't want to play with my sister's old toys."

"Thank you, Oscar. I don't know what more to say. I'll speak to my brother and I'm sure Sadie would love to come along with me."

"Fantastic, it's settled," he gave her a reassuring lop-sided grin. "Everything will be fine, Beatrice, leave it to me. I can't stay and talk, I have prior engagements to attend." He lifted the teacup to his lips and finished it with one gulp. Standing to his feet, he bobbed his head and said, "enjoy the tea. I look forward to meeting your niece," and left the parlour.

A warmth of relief seeped from her heart and trickled over her skin. Oscar was always kind to her and joy filled her imagining having Sadie with her at work.

6

COURAGE AND TROUBLE

"Are you ready, Sadie?" Beatrice said with a proud smile. Excitement welled within her heart. This was going to be the first time taking her niece to work. Wisps of dark curls escaped her cap and her glistening eyes betrayed her anxiety.

"Yes, Auntie Bea," her dainty voice warbled.

"It'll be fine," said Beatrice, leaning forward and tucking the curls behind her ears. "You'll love it. You've never seen a house so fancy. It's huge and shiny."

"Can't I go to school or stay home? My friends will walk with me," the little girl's face pinched.

"No, you can't. You're too young to stay on your own. If anything bad happened to you, I'd never forgive myself."

Unlike Sadie at this age, Beatrice had had Roy to take her to school and look after her; that is when he attended school.

Sadie's cheeks dimpled as a weak smile stretched across her face and she nodded.

"Let's hurry or we'll be late," Beatrice said.

Lifting her bag over her shoulder, Beatrice grabbed Sadie's hand and they left the tenement. The streets were busy with carts on the move, horses cantering with carriages hitched to them and merchants claiming to passers-by their wares were the best in town.

The stagecoach pulled to the side and the driver hollered for passengers. Beatrice quickened her steps clutching Sadie's hand. Panting, she paid the fee and helped Sadie inside.

Beatrice smiled watching Sadie lean against the window staring at the activities beyond the window. The stagecoach crossed over the bridge, and the little girl's eyes widened like saucers.

"The water is dark and scary," Sadie said, glancing at Beatrice. "What if we fall in?"

Chortling, Beatrice rubbed her back. "It's safe in here. We won't fall in."

From the darkness of Southwark, the world transformed into a visionary spectrum of colours as the sun shone through the window. Passing rows of well-kept houses with trimmed flowery gardens Beatrice smiled at Sadie's *aah's* admiring the houses until the stagecoach stopped at Kennington Lane where they climbed out.

Holding Sadie's hand, they walked towards the Talloway house.

"Sadie, there are some rules you need to remember. Whenever we enter, we must be quiet and not talk to anyone unless someone from the family or butler talks to us. Even though you're young, I'll teach you how to clean."

"Is it hard, Auntie Bea?"

"No, at first you might find it hard because you're little, but the more you work the easier it will get." Beatrice noticed the Talloway gate. "Hush, now, the butler's name is Mr Burkes and that is what you call him. I don't think he'll talk to you, though."

Beatrice knocked on the door as she always did, but her

heart pounded in her head. Did Oscar tell Mr Burkes she'd be bringing Sadie? She didn't want trouble and it would upset Sadie if he was in a mood.

The door opened and Sadie clutched Beatrice shaking beneath the butler's concentrated stare.

His mouth tugged upward creating an unfamiliar expression on his face as his face wrinkled.

"Ah, Miss Portly, I believe this is the young one Mr Talloway spoke of?"

"Yes, my niece, Sadie," said Beatrice, who whispered in her niece's ear, "Stand up and greet Mr Burkes."

Still clutching Beatrice, she straightened her body and said in an unsteady, but polite voice, "Good day, Mr Burkes."

His pencil-thin moustache lifted and he opened the door wider.

"Come inside or you'll catch a death of a cold."

Dipping her head, Beatrice hurried Sadie inside blocking her eyes from the painting in the hallway."

"Mr Talloway has had a room prepared for the young Miss Portly."

"Thank you, that's kind of him, but it's not necessary."

"Very well, in case you change your mind, it's the second room to the right on this level," he said. After one last glance at Sadie, he swivelled on his heels and left them alone.

"Come," Beatrice said and led her towards the maid's room where she dressed into her cleaning uniform.

"It's a pretty dress," Sadie said, rubbing the fabric between her fingers.

"It's comfortable to clean in, but pretty..." Beatrice stopped noticing the awe on Sadie's face. Hunching down she placed her hand over her niece's shoulder. "Would you like me to ask Mr Talloway to get one for you?"

Her eyes lit up. "You can do that?"

"Uh-huh," Beatrice nodded with a smile. "You'll need to help me clean though."

Sadie clapped her hands together, and said, "Yes, I want to clean with you."

"Today, just watch what I do, alright?"

Sadie's head bobbed.

Beatrice led her to the study, bid her niece to sit on a chair and started cleaning. Sadie began to softly hum and Beatrice smiled. There was no one around to mind. Mr Burkes had his duties and would leave them alone.

"What a beautiful song," Oscar said, leaning against the door with a bright smile.

Sadie stopped humming and paled. She jumped off the chair and ran to Beatrice, using her as a shield.

"Don't be silly," Beatrice said, turning to face her niece.

"It's quite fine," said Oscar sauntering inside with his hands behind his back. Walking towards them, he bent down and held out his hand. Sadie dug her face into the folds of Beatrice's dress.

"Oh dear," Oscar said, amused. He pulled his hand away. "I suppose I'd better find someone else who will eat these sweets."

Sadie's head whipped over and eyed Oscar and his outstretched hand with a small bag of hard-boiled sweets.

"I... I like sweets," Sadie responded with a quick glance at Beatrice, who nodded.

"Then take them. They're all yours. See, I do not need them." He patted his stomach. "If I eat any more I'll have a stomachache."

A wide smile crinkled Sadie's face as she took the bag. "Thank you, sir."

"Oscar, you shouldn't have," said Beatrice, admiration growing in her heart. Why was he kind to her? He always went out of his way to speak to her and offered advice asking questions about her life.

"As I said," he winked. "If I eat any more I'll get sick."

Sadie giggled and returned to her chair, sucking on a sweet.

"My niece has decided to help me clean and would a dress like mine," Beatrice said, pride and warmth swelling in her chest. "She's little, but would you be happy with her cleaning?"

"She'll be helping you?" Oscar shrugged. "I don't see a problem getting her a uniform if that's what she wants."

Sadie's head bobbed faster than a bandalore.

"That's settled," Oscar said with a smile rising along one side of his face. "Next time you come here, young Miss Portly, you can have a dress like your aunt."

"Sh..sa..shie," Sadie responded sucking the sweet.

Oscar glimpsed at Beatrice with a confused frown.

"She wants you to call her Sadie," Beatrice said with a light-hearted chuckle. "Sadie don't talk with food in your mouth."

"Sorry," she said, popping another sweet into her mouth.

"Good to see you again, Beatrice," Oscar said and turned to Sadie. "I've been eager to meet you and thank you for eating my sweets. You saved me."

Sadie beamed at him and nodded.

Beatrice flushed as Oscar stared at her. Clearing his throat, he said, "I'll leave you to it. I have a meeting to attend soon."

"I like him," Sadie remarked when Oscar had left the room.

Nodding her head, Beatrice stayed silent; as her niece pointed it out, so did she.

∼

THE DAYS BEGAN TURNING DARKER and Beatrice hurried Sadie through the streets of Southwark. She guessed Roy would be home by now and hoped he'd bought the supplies she requested to cook supper.

Worry for her brother set in her heart. Since Tilly's death, he'd returned to bottles of whiskey rising late every morning with a booming headache. She hoped he didn't have a bad day at the docks, otherwise as the night progressed his temper would gradually turn sour and he'd become argumentative until he passed out.

The wind whistled past their ears and Beatrice heard Sadie shiver. Pulling her closer, Beatrice shielded her niece from the biting air. From her earnings, she decided to buy Sadie a new coat. She couldn't guess where Roy spent his money other than partial rent, food, and drink

"Nearly home, Sadie," Beatrice said, her heart full of pity towards her brave niece.

"Should we have roast duck tonight?" Beatrice teased, helping Sadie inside the tenement.

Giggling, Sadie answered, "Only with china plates and red wine, Auntie Bea."

"Good girl," Beatrice laughed, noting how Sadie enjoyed their imaginary game. It helped to pass the time and Beatrice tried all she could to divert Sadie's attention from the traumatic loss of Tilly, and by the looks of things; her father, too.

When they arrived at their room, the distasteful smell of sweet and sour fruit combined with damp grass and timber wafted through the air.

"I don't like that smell," said Sadie following close behind Beatrice, who sighed.

"Oi, fina... ya back... took long," Roy said, slouched across the couch with a half-empty bottle of whiskey in his hand. On the floor, there was an empty bottle of whiskey.

"Oh, Roy. Why must you drink?" Beatrice said trying to

hide her disappointment. He looked away pretending to not hear her as she placed her bag near the table.

Beatrice faced him with a sigh, "Did you get the groceries I asked?"

"Yeah," he hiccupped. Peering at Sadie, he lamented, "Ain't ya going to give ya dad a hug? I mithed… missed you."

Sadie glanced at Beatrice with reservation, but she shuffled towards her father and leaned over giving him a weak hug.

"Ya was good at those rich people's house, yeah?"

"Yes, Daddy, I was good," Sadie's cheeks dimpled as she tried to smile. "The kind man will give me a dress like Auntie Bea."

"Kind man? Dress, what dress?" he said in an accusational tone.

"Oh, relax," Beatrice said, digging for a pot inside the cupboard which once had a chipped door. It now leaned against the paint-chipped wall. "Sadie wants to help me clean and asked for a uniform. My employer said he'd get her one."

"Huh?" Roy sat up with a scowl on his face. "No daughter of mine will clean a rich man's house."

"There's nothing wrong with that. It's honest work," Beatrice said, shooting an angry look in his direction. "What do you think I've been doing all these years? What do you think Auntie Sadie was doing for *us*?"

"I want to, Daddy," Sadie said, sitting beside him. "I watched Auntie Bea and she was happy. It looks fun."

Roy stared at her with a raised brow causing lines to form across his forehead.

"Fun?" He took a drink of whiskey and roared with laughter. "Now, if Tilly were here, she'd find that funny, too. Her daughter cleaning houses," he mocked with a raucous laugh.

Tears brimmed Sadie's eyes and her lower lip quivered.

"Shame on you!" Beatrice scolded him and hurried to her

niece. "Sadie, there's some water in the back room. Go wash up while I make supper."

Wiping her eyes, Sadie nodded and disappeared.

"What's wrong with you?" Beatrice was close to tears. She missed her brother. If only Tilly and their aunt had survived. "You're drinking every night and you're drunk. I'm surprised you are still working at the docks."

"Ya donn-a know anything," Roy gulped from the bottle.

"You're hurting Sadie, she needs you. When will you stop drinking? You won't find an answer there."

Roy's head lolled to one side and mumbled, "When... I stop missing... Tilly..." his voice droned softer and softer as his eyes fluttered closed.

7
DISASTER FALLING

"Why is Sadie always going to work with you?" Roy said, pulling his coat over his shoulders.

Beatrice frowned and stared at him in surprise. "It's better than to leave her at home alone. Besides, she enjoys it."

"Cleaning rich folk's houses?" he scoffed. "Running after their every whim? I can't see much fun in that, doing their beck and call," he said with a smirk. "Hoy, Sadie, I want you to come with me today. See what I do. That's real fun."

Sadie shook her head and said, "I don't want to, it's scary. It smells at the docks and there are animals," she shivered, "I think they're dead, they lie still and smell like rotten meat."

"I know you want to spend time with her, but why not take her to the park instead? Do you think the docks are a place for a young girl?" Beatrice said her heart hammering. What was Roy thinking?

"There are plenty of young kids your age," he said lifting his chin. "You can work, too. I've seen girls around working. Maybe you can work with me instead."

"It's a bad idea, Roy, I think—"

"Yeah? Go ahead and think. Remember she's my daughter. I have the say, not you."

Exhaling a deep breath, Beatrice lowered her head and gazed at the terrified expression on Sadie's ashen face.

"It's alright, you'll be fine with your dad," said Beatrice faking a reassuring smile. She glowered at her brother and stated, "No harm will come to you. Your daddy will protect you."

Roy waved his hand in the air and blew out air through his lips. "What you going on about? Of course, she's safe."

"Keep your coat on," Beatrice prodded with a quick wink at Sadie, who stared at her with a blank expression.

Beatrice walked towards Sadie and kissing her on the cheek, said, "Listen to your father and I'll see you later."

A lump formed in the back of Beatrice's throat and her heart crushed at the pain in the girl's eyes. It didn't feel right, but there was nothing she could do. Roy had the final say, not her.

Beatrice left with a heavy heart and whispered a prayer for the Lord's protection over Sadie. It was the first time, in a long time, she would clean the Talloway's house without her niece. Oscar had spread the word and all the families allowed Sadie to work alongside Beatrice. Being alone without Sadie, felt different and she questioned whether she should've fought harder with Roy about it.

When she arrived at the Talloway's house, Mr Burkes appeared to be disappointed at Sadie's absence. Beatrice knew him well enough now to know that he wasn't as good at hiding his emotions as he thought.

The day wasn't as fun and entertaining without Sadie. Beatrice missed her sweet smile and odd quirks whenever she discovered new things around the house. Thinking of the little girl spending the day at the docks sent chills down her spine. It was not a safe place for Sadie.

Beatrice brushed tendrils of hair from her face as she changed from her uniform into her clothes. Fatigue overwhelmed her and all she could think about was Sadie. Leaving the room, and closing the door behind her Oscar walked down the hallway towards her with a broad grin.

"You're leaving already?" he said, tilting his head.

"Hello, Oscar, yes, I need to get home."

"My father has dinner arrangements elsewhere and it would be lonely on my own. Would you care to join me?"

"That's kind of you, but I couldn't—"

"Please, I do enjoy your company and my sister has gone to stay with our mother. I'll be completely alone. Pity young Sadie isn't here it would've been a pleasure to have her, too."

Beatrice's cheeks turned pink and felt the blood racing through her veins. Shaking her head, she said, "I don't, well, I mean I—"

"Don't make me beg, Beatrice," he said grinning, hands against his chin, his fingers pressed together as if in prayer.

Squaring her shoulders, Beatrice responded with a smile, "Alright, I don't want you to beg. It doesn't suit you."

"Wonderful," Oscar declared. "I knew you'd accept. I've told Mr Burkes to have a place set for you."

Beatrice stared at him flabbergasted. What would Mr Burkes think about her dining with Oscar?

She followed him to the dining room and as he'd said, there were two places set; one at the head of the table, the other to the left. The wall-mounted gas lights were dimmed and a lit cylindrical candle was placed in the centre of the table.

Beatrice felt awkward. She lost count of how many times she'd cleaned this room and never imagined she'd be seated at the table eating with Oscar.

"I hope you like French onion soup," Oscar said, pulling up the chair at the head of the table. "Our cook is French and such talent is not unnoticed."

Beatrice offered a thankful smile. She'd never tasted anything other than withered vegetable soup. "It sounds delightful," she said, hoping to hide her anxiety and guilt. How could she eat a lavish meal while Sadie and Roy ate the scraps he stole from the docks?

"Where is your mother, Mrs Talloway?" Beatrice said, enjoying the soup. "I thought she lived here and spent the time with your sister." She'd never tasted anything so fresh, pure and delectable. Despite the beautiful home and its décor, Beatrice had noticed the lack of a womanly touch.

Oscar almost choked as he swallowed, patting his chest. "Excuse me, sorry," he said spluttering.

"Sorry, did I say something wrong?"

"No, not at all," he said, thanking the servant for clearing the soup plates and serving the main course; stuffed roast beef, roast chicken, an assortment of vegetables, gravy with fresh bread and platters of fruit.

"No, my mother doesn't live here and neither does my sister."

"Why?" Beatrice sipped her wine. "I'm sorry. I'm asking too many questions. It's none of my business."

"No, it's not that," Oscar said, shaking his head. "I'm sorry. It's just my father is a bit upset that my sister decided to live with our mother though I'm not surprised. I love my sister, but she is spoilt and doesn't know our mother. I'm afraid Felicia will be hurt or end up like my mother..." his voice trailed and stared at her wide-eyed. "What am I saying? Please forget all I said."

Beatrice noted the sadness in his voice. "It's alright, Oscar. If you don't want to talk about it, I understand. I know what it's like, except I never knew my parents. It was just Roy and me. Our Auntie Sadie looked after us until she died. Then we had to look after ourselves."

"I see. Well, I guess I should tell you a little then of my family," he braved a smile. Beatrice observed the pain in his eyes.

"My mother came from an esteemed, wealthy family. My parents had an arranged marriage. It was all business, you see," he said attempting a casual tone, and added beef and vegetables to his plate.

"My family's background is quite boring; actually. On my mother's side is a history of bankers, aristocrats, royalty, and the like. Because of that, my mother's family holds a ridiculous amount of wealth. My father comes from an aristocratic family with great insight into the financial market. Unfortunately, my mother was in love with someone else and she was under the impression my father was beneath her. I believe she fought the marriage betrothal and didn't succeed. After I was born, she began to have an affair with the man she loved and neglected me. My nannies were more of a mother to me."

"That's awful, Oscar. I didn't realise that wealthy people had such problems. Forgive me," Beatrice exhaled a breath of embarrassment and shame. "That came out all wrong. It's just my brother goes on about how wealthy people have perfect lives."

"Don't mention it. No harm done. My mother never treated my father or me fairly. She desired everything my father could not provide to her liking and because of the affair, she eventually came to think she could do whatever she liked." He paused for a breath. "I shouldn't say this, but recent news has come as a shock to me and my father is devastated. Felicia, as it turns out, is not my father's daughter."

Beatrice gasped and stared at him aghast. Without thinking, she placed her hand over his and said, "I'm sorry. You don't need to speak about it if it makes you uncomfortable."

"No, it's fine," he said with a bashful smile. His eyes darted to her hand and she instantly withdrew her hand, cheeks crimson.

"Do I miss her?" he said, "If that's what's on your mind, no, sadly I don't because I never knew her. I remember her face and impressive fashion, but nothing more." He reached for his glass of red wine and gulped half the glass. "The day my father discovered she'd been having an affair with the diplomat, he realised he could not live life under my mother's thumb. It was her family that ruled the roost, so to speak, and he packed up everything, me and Felicia, and we moved here. I doubt my mother showed interest in finding us at that time, but since she's claiming Felicia is not his child, he's initiated a notice of divorce." He leaned back into the chair with a sigh. "I don't think my father will ever accept that Felicia is not his daughter."

"That's awful, Oscar. I can't imagine what you must've gone through... and now, it's terrible."

"Beatrice, I didn't want to burden you with all this trouble and now," he said with a sardonic chuckle, "I'm telling you everything that I do not want to tell you. I wanted a pleasant evening and now I've ruined it."

"No, Oscar. Thank you for sharing with me. It's important that you get this off your chest and I appreciate that you trust me enough to tell me."

He stared at her in a way that made her stomach twist into a pleasant knot and she momentarily lost her breath.

"Thank you," he said flashing a genuine smile. "I do feel better for it, but I'm embarrassed to have told you all that I did."

"Have you spoken with her?"

"No, and I don't think I ever will. She isn't interested in me and I don't mind. As I said, I don't miss her. How can I if I never knew her?" Sadness crawled over his face. "Now that Felicia is gone, my father is reminded about the rumours he heard about my mother gallivanting across the cities of Birmingham with the diplomat. He'd defended her honour and denied every cruel word that had been said about her. As we speak, he is holed up in his study with gin and tonic, perhaps whisky, I'm not sure. Mr Burkes has assured me he'll keep watch over my father."

"I don't know what to say," Beatrice blinked back tears as his sorrow washed over her. "Do you want me to leave?"

Oscar's head whipped up. "Goodness, no. Please stay. I'm glad he decided to move here," he tilted his head with an enchanting smile. "We're both happier here and I got to meet you."

Beatrice flushed.

"I came to the conclusion that I would never let anyone walk all over me, even if they are family. It isn't right," he said with a determination in his voice that moved Beatrice's heart. "I hope to one day purchase a house in the countryside, away from the hustle and bustle of nosy, wealthy people with oversized egos that could flatten this country."

She joined him in laughter, relieved that his sense of humour had returned. "If my father heard me talk this way, he'd reprimand me. I feel I can trust you, Beatrice," he said, gazing at her with wild, but heartfelt eyes. "It's been years since I've trusted anyone."

"I'm honoured, thank you," Beatrice said, returning his stare in awe. Her heart beat faster falling into his majestic eyes. How did he come to trust her like this? They barely knew one another and yet he opened up his life in complete confidence.

But, it was more than that. He made her feel something she didn't understand. Was it the same for him?

Taking a deep breath, she responded, "Life for me has been different from yours," and offered a weak smile. How could she explain the vast difference between living in the slums and a neighbourhood like Kennington? However, they both understood pain.

"I've told you a lot about my life and Roy has always been the decision-maker. He was my big brother and I always looked up to him, even when he was wrong. I let him walk all over me and even now... sometimes I don't know what I'm doing."

"You seem sure of yourself. You're self-reliant and the way you take care of Sadie is admirable." A smile rose to the side of his handsome face. "She looks up to you. Anyone can see that."

"She misses her mother, Tilly. Since she passed away, Roy has been unbearable and refuses to stop drinking. I try to stand up to him, but he won't listen," Beatrice sighed. "I think he forgets that Sadie misses her mother, too. When he's had too much to drink his temper turns foul. I've had to rescue him from taverns on occasion. Sometimes he's arrived home black and blue blaming others for starting a row."

"I know he's your brother, but he sounds like a dangerous character. Are you safe living with him?" Oscar stared at her with concern, his smile fading. "Mind my asking, but... has he ever... hurt either of you?"

Beatrice froze and her blood turned cold, a feeling of dread spread from the pit of her stomach. What if Roy started drinking with Sadie in his care? What if he forgot about her and something happened?

"What's wrong? You've turned pale. Is the food not to your liking?"

"No, the meal was delicious. I'm fine, but please excuse me,

Oscar, I must go home." Beatrice said, offering a polite smile. "I enjoyed spending this time with you," she breathed a small chuckle, "We even bared our souls."

"If I've offended you, I apologise. Please don't go," his voice was troubled and his brows knitted as his soulful eyes stared at her.

When she rose to her feet, he stood and kept his eyes fixed on her with a bewildered expression.

"Thank you for inviting me to dinner it was kind of you, but I must leave before it gets darker. Roy took Sadie with him to the docks. If I don't leave now it will be difficult to find my way home through the streets in the dark and there is not much light. They'll wonder where I am."

Oscar exhaled what sounded like relief. "I understand. Thank you for joining me tonight, Beatrice, even though I was melancholy," he said with a thankful smile. "You're right, it is getting dark and I shouldn't keep you. My driver will take you home. I won't accept no for an answer. My carriage is already prepared."

"Thank you," Beatrice smiled. He walked with her to the front door, waiting at the front of the house was a carriage. It was as though he'd planned it.

"I appreciate you staying here," he said and turned to face her. Taking her by surprise, he grasped her hand and lifted it to his mouth, lifting his eyes to make eye contact, he kissed the top of her hand and her body flushed as her skin tingled.

Beatrice was elated but thankful for the darkness to hide her crimson face. "I... Well, uh—"

"I know, you need to go," he said with a satisfied smile. "You'll be safe with my driver."

Beatrice nodded, speechless, thanked him again and hurried towards the carriage with her hand pressed against her cheek.

8

FOOD FOR THOUGHT

Beatrice thanked the driver and closed the carriage door. Racing up the staircase, she heard Roy's voice before she reached the second floor. The same dread from earlier overcame her and she quickened her steps, almost tripping up the staircase.

Slamming her shoulder against the door, it creaked open and she gagged at the sickly sweet, malty smell in the air. Her eyes widened, staring at Sadie slumped on the floor, sobbing. Roy towered over her, forefinger in the air, yelling. In his left hand was a half-empty bottle of alcohol. Circling his feet were two empty bottles of alcohol. One appeared to have fallen and spilled over.

Sadness swelled in her heart. It was as she feared. Beatrice dropped her bag and raced to her brother, pushing him away from Sadie.

"What's going on?" she demanded, staring at her brother in fury. Waves of anger flowed through her body.

"I lost my job!" Roy yelled with a hint of a slur. "I told her not to go near the warehouse. Where did she go? The warehouse and my boss got angry. He said she should not have come to the dock. Not a... place for children, he said... but, boys work from age five..."

"Calm down, Roy," Beatrice reached for the bottle in hopes of taking it away from him, but he slapped her hand away scowling and stared as if daring her to try again.

"Stop it. Your drinking is the problem... Look at your daughter, Sadie, she's—"

Thwack. The sound reverberated in the room and Roy's eyes grew like Auntie Sadie's untouched saucers and he backed away, shaking his head. The bottle slipped from his hand and crashed to the floor, glass shards scattered across the floor.

"I'm sorry... Bea, I'm... I'm..." his warbled voice was full of confusion.

With tears in her eyes, Beatrice rubbed her cheek, gazing at her brother in pity as he raced to the room he and Tilly used to share.

Beatrice glanced at Sadie sniffling, still sitting on the floor, and sat beside her.

"Everything will be alright," Beatrice said in a soothing tone and wrapped her arms around Sadie. "Daddy is not thinking right. It's the whiskey that's talking."

Sadie's eyes glistened as she stared at Beatrice. "But, he hit you. He's wrong. Is your cheek hurting?"

"It stings," Beatrice managed a weak smile, hoping there'd be no bruising. "But my heart is hurting more."

"Why is your heart sore?"

"I don't like to see you cry," Beatrice stroked Sadie's arm. "And, your dad isn't thinking clearly."

Tears rolled down Sadie's smooth skin. "Does Daddy not love me anymore?"

"Of course, he does. He loves you so much." Beatrice said, holding her close. Ignoring the throbbing that rose to her left eye, she added, "He is hurt, too, but that doesn't mean what he's doing is right. I love your daddy, because he's my brother and I'm sad he's acting this way. I want him and you to be happy."

"Did Daddy lose his job because I went to see the pretty clothes?"

"No, your dad should have let you come with me. His boss was angry at him for going to work late every day and I'm sure his boss could smell the alcohol. I don't go to the dock, but I know it's not a place for children. Maybe he hasn't worked like he used to do."

"Is... Is it true that Mommy died because... of me?" Sadie's voice distorted and tears gushed from her eyes. "Daddy said... it's me... I did it... did I make her sick?"

Beatrice glimpsed at the broken bottle of whiskey with the liquid seeping into the soggy wood.

"Your Mommy got sick because that's what happens to people. It's no one's fault, especially not yours."

Beatrice gripped her niece as if she were about to float away. "I won't let anything happen to you, Sadie. I'll protect you always. Why don't you sleep next to me tonight? You wash up your face and climb into my bed. I'll get the fire warmed up and clean up the mess. When I'm finished I'll come and lie next to you."

You promise?" Sadie hiccupped as she wiped the tears from her eyes.

"Yes," Beatrice said with a nod. Feigning a smile, she watched her niece scramble into bed and fall fast asleep before Beatrice began to stoke the hearth.

∼

Beatrice woke to Roy's groans slamming against the walls. The thumping from his room indicated he'd risen from his bed, hands clamouring for something to hold onto.

She moved and a bundle of heat snuggled next to her. Poking her niece, Beatrice said, "Time to get up, Sadie."

At the whining sound, Beatrice slid her hands beneath the covers and began to tickle the sides of Sadie's tummy.

"No," Sadie yelped, her body writhing as she giggled. "I'll get up! I will... promise..." she gasped between bouts of laughter.

Grinning, Beatrice released her and lifted the blankets. "What's for breakfast?"

"Grilled potatoes and gravy," Sadie beamed, but her jaw dropped staring at her aunt. "Auntie Bea, you're..." she exhaled. "Your eye, it's black and red. It's swollen." She bit on her quivering lip.

"Oh, it's nothing," Beatrice said with a warm smile, ignoring the throbbing pain from her eye and along her cheek. "You say it's swollen? Don't worry, I think some cool water will do the trick."

Beatrice couldn't tell Sadie that she could barely see through her left eye. She glanced at Roy stumbling from his room and sighed.

"Potatoes and scrambled eggs," Beatrice said, holding Sadie's attention. "What do you think about that for breakfast and mystery meat?"

"Don't tease," Sadie pouted, her eyes fixed on Beatrice's face. "We don't have sausages."

"Did someone say... sausages," Roy said his voice a mumble of words. He stopped short and stared at Beatrice, who had climbed out of bed and was walking towards the kitchen cupboard.

Sadie's face pinched and she pointed at Beatrice. "Look at what you did, Daddy. You hurt Auntie Bea."

"Don't talk that way to your father," Beatrice said over her shoulder, digging for a pan.

"No, Sadie's right," said Roy, guilt falling across his face. He slumped onto the couch and hung his head in shame. "I'm sorry, Bea. I-I always swore to protect you... I didn't... I'm sorry," he said, lifting his head and staring at Beatrice with a rueful expression. "I've been a terrible brother and father, I'm going to change. Stop drinking alcohol and change my behaviour. I promise."

He glanced at Sadie with a splotchy face and said, "I'm sorry. I miss Mommy so much that I forgot you miss her you, too."

Tears rolled down Sadie's cheeks and she ran to her father embracing him. "I do, too, and I miss you, Daddy."

"I'll be a better, dad," he said. "I'm going to speak to my boss and ask for my job back. Maybe I was wrong. I thought he was trying to find a way to get rid of me. It's not your fault for anything, Sadie, it's my fault. Drinking too much made me a bad worker and I was making mistakes all the time."

"Can we go on walks again and have a picnic like we used to?" Sadie's voice held earnest and optimism.

"Yes, let's do that again. You and me."

"Can Auntie Bea come with us?"

Glancing at Beatrice, Roy nodded, "Yes, she must come, too."

Beatrice's heart melted, but she held reservations in the back of her mind. Her brother meant well, but he lacked the resolve to keep his promises.

"I'm sure you'll get your job back," Beatrice said, offering a comforting smile through the doubts that swam through her mind. "If not, there are other places you can find work."

Roy appeared to ignore her and turned his full attention onto Sadie. While he sat with Sadie telling her stories about working at the docks and how he'd convince his boss to take him back, Beatrice prepared their breakfast.

∼

A WEEK HAD PASSED since Roy promised to change his ways and while he continued to look for work, she struggled to put food on the table. His boss at the dock didn't want to take Roy back for lack of trust and poor performance. After three days of no employment success, Roy resumed drinking alcohol again and gradually became foul-tempered.

"I'm getting better at polishing, Auntie Bea," Sadie said in her black dress covered by a pinafore with ruffled trimming. She grinned as she polished the parlour table. "I can see my face."

Smiling with a cheerful side glance, Beatrice chuckled and gave her a thumbs-up sign. She was delighted that Sadie's discouragement had transformed into enthusiasm, despite Roy's uncontrollable mood swings.

Familiar footsteps headed into the room and Oscar greeted them with a bright grin and a plate of colourful sugar biscuits.

"Help yourself," he told Sadie, who eyed the plate with great interest.

Beatrice nodded and Sadie grabbed a biscuit with a polite, "Thank you."

"Oh, what happened to your eye?" Oscar said, scrutinising her face. "There's a bit of swelling around your eye."

"It's nothing," Beatrice said with a nervous chuckle and a dismissive wave. "It doesn't hurt," she lied. She couldn't tell anyone it felt as though a stack of bricks had fallen into her face.

"It doesn't look like nothing," he said.

"Really, it's nothing to be poked up about. I was in a rush at home cooking and I tripped over a chair," she said, avoiding eye contact. "Just a bump on the corner of the couch."

"I see," he appeared unconvinced, "it seems much more serious than a bump from a piece of furniture."

He glanced at Sadie. She opened her mouth, but with one firm look from Beatrice, Sadie bit on another biscuit.

Beatrice didn't answer.

With one last glance at her, he seized pushing the topic and offered Beatrice a biscuit. "You better take one before Sadie and I eat them all. I confess..." he said, hands up in the air, "guilty as charged in having a sweet tooth."

"You like sweets, too?" Sadie stared at him, pleased to be munching on another biscuit.

"Love them," he said. "Our cook gets most frustrated whenever I sneak into the kitchen and help myself to a plate of iced biscuits."

"Like this one?" Sadie giggled

"Yes," he returned with a light chuckle. "I'll fetch more later when she's out to buy more ingredients. She's baking for my father's guests this evening. Thankfully, I don't need to attend."

"Can I come to one of your parties?" Sadie said, to Beatrice's horror.

"Hush, you need to keep cleaning, Sadie," Beatrice said, her cheeks pink. When did Sadie become so brazen?

"Oh, it's alright," Oscar responded, a smile rising up his cheek. "Yes, perhaps someday I'll have a party for you."

Giggling, Sadie chose another biscuit before retrieving her cloths. Turning to face Oscar she said, "Mr Talloway, would you like to have supper with us?"

Beatrice paused and blanched. Sadie's words were like a

blow to the stomach. What was she thinking? Having Oscar at their home was ridiculous. Why would he want to visit their degraded home? They didn't live in the best neighbourhood either.

"Auntie Bea cooks well, delicious actually. It will be my birthday soon and I'm going to have a roast beef." Sadie gave her aunt a proud grin.

"I'm sorry, Oscar, she doesn't know what she's saying—"

"Yes, I do, Auntie, it's my birthday…"

"Don't interrupt," Beatrice said. "You know better. Where are your manners?"

"Sorry," Sadie said, heaving a sigh of defeat and pushing the remains of the biscuit into her mouth. Her shoulders stooped as she began to dust the window sills.

"Nonsense, I'd love to come have supper with you. Especially for your birthday," he emphasised his last few words and a smile returned to Sadie's face.

Beatrice stood upright, her fingers playing with the ruffles of her pinafore, and said, "Uh, the roast beef is exaggerated…" She drew in a breath as heat coursed up her neck to her cheeks. "You see my brother is out of work and…" she stared at Sadie's fading smile and her heart clenched with shame. She had hoped to surprise Sadie with a chocolate cake from the baker around the corner from where they lived.

"No, Beatrice, I must insist. I know you've been having a rough time. Let this be my gift to young Sadie," he said, and digging into his pocket, he pulled out a wad of notes. Handing them to Beatrice, he said, "Can't disappoint the girl on her special day." He grinned. "Besides, I'd like to taste your delicious roast beef."

Beatrice's eyes widened and wished the ground would swallow her up. She'd never seen so much money before and decided she couldn't take Oscar's money, but he persisted with a determination she could not refuse.

"Okay, how about Saturday evening?" she said and grimaced thinking of Roy knowing he would not be happy. "Her birthday is on Sunday, but we go to church in the morning and she's going to play with friends afterwards."

"Sounds brilliant," he waggled his brows at a delighted Sadie, who was chewing on the tips of her fingers. "I can't wait. I'm excited already."

"Yes, it... will be wonderful to have you visit us," Beatrice said with a tight-lipped smile, hoping he wouldn't notice her apprehension.

Oscar picked up the empty plate, full of crumbs, and excused himself before leaving the room. Beatrice turned her head to face Sadie, and her scolding words left her as she listened to her niece humming as she swiped the cloth against the window casings.

Feeling the world on her shoulders, Beatrice left Sadie to finish cleaning the room while she headed towards the study dreading what Roy might say. Dread filled her bones every time she glanced at the grandfather clock in the hallway. With every second that passed, meant she'd have to face Roy with the news.

Beatrice struggled as she attempted enthusiasm as they bid farewell to Mr Burkes, who knew all about the Saturday arrangement thanks to Sadie's animated prattling.

"Do you think Dad will be happy," Sadie said, holding Beatrice's hand.

"I don't know. He's been in a mood lately and," she glimpsed at her niece's hopeful stare. "He might surprise us. He could enjoy Oscar's company because he's a nice person."

Beatrice didn't know what to tell Sadie. She recalled the

conversation she'd had with Roy two nights ago over his drinking. Sadie had been sound asleep.

"There's a hole in my chest," he'd said in a drunken state, slouching over the couch with an empty whiskey bottle in his hand, stinking up the windowless room. "It won't go away and the pain gets worse. Whiskey helps take it away, mostly."

He'd passed out before she could talk any sense into him. Perhaps she could dissuade him from drinking on Saturday night.

"Daddy, Daddy," Sadie yelled as the front door scraped open with a high-pitched whine. "Guess who's coming for supper on Saturday?"

Roy stared at her with a raised brow. "Huh? What you talking about?"

"I invited Mr Talloway to have supper with us. He wants to cause it's my birthday. He gave Auntie Bea extra money to get roast beef, pudding and…"

"He's giving you charity money now?" Roy said rising from the couch and glaring at Beatrice through hazy eyes. "What's going on?"

"Your daughter's birthday is on Sunday and she wants my boss's son to have supper with us. He is coming whether you like it or not."

"Rich folks think they own everything, don't they?" he scoffed, taking a sip from the empty bottle and tossing it onto the floor. "Even think they can take over someone's home."

"You're overreacting," Beatrice clicked her tongue as she picked up the bottle from the floor. "It will be fun and Sadie is excited about her birthday. I'm sure you can spare her that little treat, can't you?"

Roy waved his hand in the air with a grunt of disapproval, wriggled to his feet and swaggered into his room.

9
ON THE RUN

Saturday could not arrive fast enough for Sadie. She couldn't talk about anything else, which got on Roy's nerves. Beatrice didn't mind, she found the idea of Oscar visiting them for a change, was exciting.

"Why would someone like him want to come here, anyway?" he complained. "He's got a fancy house already."

"Sadie's won a lot of hearts," Beatrice offered a content smile. "Every house I clean love having her around."

"See her as charity, do they?"

"It's not like that at all, you know it," Beatrice said, steadying the anger that began to swell inside her. "Not every rich person is arrogant and selfish. Most of the people are kind and look how much they've given us. And, it's not because we're poor. None of them know where we live."

"Hmm," Roy snorted, one side of his nose twitched. "Not this bloke coming here. He knows where we live and will laugh at us."

"Oscar isn't like that—"

"Oh, by first name, is it now?" he said, voice rising in mockery. "Is there something I should know? What'll it be now? Hats and new dresses?" and spluttered with a scowl, "If I didn't know any better, him and you—"

"Stop it!" Beatrice couldn't contain her anger. "Don't say it and you know better than that. It's Mr Talloway to you unless he gives you permission to call him by his name. You understand?" she said, rattling through the cupboard. "If you don't mind I need to finish up Sadie's birthday supper and you're distracting me." She handed him a list. "Please go get these items from the shop and if you bring a bottle of whiskey, I'll throw it out the window."

Roy sniffed, "The one that doesn't open?"

"It will open if you bring a bottle of poison."

She inhaled a deep breath as her brother scampered away. It was a good excuse to get rid of him for a bit. Roy didn't know what he was talking about and had never met Oscar before. To think Oscar would be interested in her was absurd. The mere idea was ridiculous. Why would he, an esteemed gentleman from Kennington, ever be attracted to someone like her, who lived in Southwark?

Beatrice shook her head. Oscar was too good of a man to fall victim to another scandal after his mother's antics. Despite how she felt about him, she would never allow his reputation to be tarnished.

As Roy returned with the ingredients—and no bottle of whiskey—Oscar arrived holding a bag of hard-boiled sweets and a beautiful porcelain doll with dark brown curls. "For the birthday girl," he beamed with a lop-sided grin. "It reminded me of you."

"She's beautiful, thank you!" Sadie said with a radiant smile and hugged Oscar to Roy's disgust.

"You shouldn't have," Beatrice said with a pleased glance from Sadie to Oscar.

"What's a birthday without a gift?"

Sadie sat in the middle of the floor pretending to feed sweets to the doll, who she called 'Molly'.

Beatrice introduced Roy and Oscar, who invited Roy to address him by his first name.

"We're all human beings," Oscar said and didn't appear bothered by their dilapidated home or show signs of being sullied coming to this part of London.

While Beatrice continued cooking, she noticed the dark looks from Roy when Oscar sat on the couch—the springs poking through the unravelling upholstery—and chatted with Sadie.

"Smells delicious," Oscar said with a wink at Sadie, who sat beside him, holding her doll.

"See? I told you. Auntie Bea cooks better than your cook."

"Sadie!" Beatrice scolded.

Roy lifted his head back and guffawed.

"It's fine," Oscar smiled and responded to Sadie. "You're probably right. I don't like her vegetables. They taste bad."

Sadie nodded and said, covering her mouth with her hand, "Don't tell Auntie Bea, I don't want to hurt her feelings, but her vegetables aren't nice either."

Suppressing a laugh, Beatrice declared supper was ready and would be served on their living room table.

Beatrice noticed a scowl on her brother's face. "I'm not hungry. You all go ahead, I'll eat later," he said, and as he headed towards his room he muttered under his breath, for all to hear, "as if I'd ever eat with a toff."

Beatrice's hands clenched and she calmed her staggered breathing. How dare her brother embarrass them all like that and glared at him with fury.

"I apologise for my brother's outburst," Beatrice could

barely say the words. "He's not in his right mind being that he lost his job and has taken it badly."

"Understandable," Oscar said with a mild smile, his face ashen.

Ignoring her brother, Beatrice set the table with the roast beef, potatoes and vegetables. "Please go ahead and help yourself."

Sadie rose to her feet and raced after her father. "Daddy, come. Supper's ready and Auntie Bea's made me roast beef with gravy."

The curtain moved and Roy walked into the living room with a rugged expression on his face. Beatrice noticed his arms and hands were shaking.

"I'm sorry, Sadie," he smiled, giving her a one-armed hug. "Daddy's been going through a hard time, but you're right. It's your birthday and I want to eat your special meal."

"Now everyone is here," Beatrice said. Taking her seat, she lifted her hands and said, "Let's say grace."

Holding hands, everyone closed their eyes while Beatrice thanked the Lord for their meal.

"Daddy, Mr Talloway lives in a big house and it has a pretty garden with flowers. There are baby birds now and they call for food all the time."

"Is that so?" Roy's eyes darted at Oscar with a dark look.

"Beatrice, this is delicious. Sadie is correct in saying you're better than my cook." Oscar's lips tugged into a smile.

"Does it taste any different with porcelain or china?" Roy said glaring at him with a sardonic smile. "What about silverware?"

Closing her eyes, Beatrice held her breath.

"Oh, you're silly, Daddy," said Sadie, grinning at him. "They're polished and put away."

"Of course, they are," Roy muttered under his breath.

Lifting his chin, Oscar laughed and rewarded Sadie with a broad grin, showing teeth. "Yes, the silverware is put away, but we use them every day," he said cutting through the meat on his plate. "As far as the taste goes, it doesn't matter what cutlery is used. It depends on the efforts of the cook."

Beatrice opened her eyes and her cheeks flushed when she met Oscar's gaze and her heart thumped when he smiled.

Oscar turned to Sadie and said, "Do you go to school?"

"I did, but..." Sadie's mouth twisted into a half-smile and scrunched her face. "I clean houses now with Auntie Bea to help bring in money."

"You need extra money? Why?"

"Cause Daddy doesn't work at the docks anymore."

"Sadie!" Roy said, slamming his cup onto the table, and hissed, "He's posh, he don't care, is none of his business anyway. We're fine."

Oscar left his utensils on his plate and lifted his hands into the air. Inclining his chin, he stared at Roy and said, "I can help. I know a few people at the docks and could put in a good word for you. They are always looking for people to work down there. Is it true that children work there?"

"Yeah, it is. And, I don't need your charity," Roy said, slamming his fist onto the table. He stood to his feet, his face blood-red. "I've always done things my way. This is my house and I want you out of my house." Pointing a finger at Beatrice, he yelled, "It's your fault he's here. Don't clean his house anymore. I don't want his money paying for us."

"Stop it, Roy, you have no say in what I do and you can't act this way. You're being rude," Beatrice said pressing her lips together. "Have you forgotten it's Sadie's birthday and she invited Oscar, as her guest."

"Yes... and that, too! Stay away from my daughter," Roy

roared, glowering at Oscar with his fist shaking in the air. "You have no business being here."

"But... but, Daddy...."

Oscar's mouth set in a straight line and he dipped his head. "I'm sorry. It wasn't my intention to upset anyone," he said and turned to Sadie, whose face was tear-stained. "Thank you for inviting me. I will not forget your kindness. I hope to see you soon and a happy birthday for tomorrow."

"Don't count on it," Roy growled as the corner of his lip and nose twitched in contempt.

Without another word, Oscar stood to his feet and after struggling with the door, exited the tenement. Beatrice stared at her brother, astonished and disgusted, sickened to her stomach at her brother's actions.

"How could you..." Beatrice started but was at a loss for words. "Roy, you...."

Enraged and cussing, Roy stormed out, banging the door behind him.

Sinking into the couch, Beatrice glanced at Sadie, who was bawling and wiping her eyes.

"What did... did I do?" Sadie cried. "I made Daddy angry by bringing Mr Talloway. It's my fault, isn't it, Auntie Bea?" she sniffled. "Will he hurt Mr Talloway?"

Beatrice rose and sat beside Sadie, wrapping her arm around her shoulders and giving a tight squeeze. "No, it's not your fault. I'm sorry, Sadie, but Daddy was wrong to act that way towards Oscar."

Sadie nodded with a downcast expression. "Yes, but Mr Talloway will never come to visit me again."

"He doesn't blame you. It's not your fault."

"Daddy was never angry like this," she shivered, "I don't want him to hurt you again." Tears filled her eyes and she sobbed. "Why is... is... he always... angry at me. I wa-ant... Mommy back."

Beatrice remained silent and agreed with Sadie. Neither of them knew where Roy had gone, but she suspected where he might have gone. It was still early for taverns to be open. If only she hadn't relied on Roy so much when they were younger and spent most of her time cleaning houses then perhaps she'd have more friends. Fear rushed through her veins at the thought of her brother's return in his foul temper.

"Sadie, you know what happens when Daddy becomes this angry, don't you?"

"Yes," she nodded, wiping her face with her hands and sleeves.

"I think we should pack a bag and leave until Daddy calms down. I don't know where we can go other than the church on Friar Street. I think they have a shelter."

"Will we be safe?"

"Of course, I would never take you anywhere that would put you in danger." Beatrice pulled her niece into a tight embrace.

"I'll go where you go," answered Sadie with a sniff.

"Good, now go wash your face and pack up your clothes. We must hurry before Daddy comes back. We'll come back when he's calmer."

∼

BEATRICE FOUND two bags and they both packed their clothes and other items. Oscar's face crossed her mind and she shook her head. No, even in their moment of desperation, they couldn't go to his house. She was his cleaner and she was certain it wouldn't be proper.

"Let's go," Beatrice whispered and waved her hand for

Sadie to follow as they snuck out the door. The walls were paper thin and by morning everyone would know what had happened and over time, Roy's tempered voice would have reached the sixth floor.

Rushing out of the tenement, they turned right towards Southwark Street, but Beatrice stopped in her tracks; Sadie bounced into her.

"It's Daddy!" Sadie said in a panic-stricken voice.

"We're going to have to turn around through Mint Street," Beatrice whispered.

With Roy swaggering towards them, she didn't think they had a choice. It wasn't a safe route, but it would take them to the main road and onto Friar. They tip-toed past their tenement only a few feet away from her brother, Sadie's foot slipped and knocked over a tin can; clanging as it rolled down the street.

Beatrice noticed him look up and he swore, picking up his pace.

"Hoy, where'd you think you're... going?" His voice sliced through the silent air as he attempted to grasp Sadie's arm.

"Run, Sadie," Beatrice said as panic flowed from her chest to her voice. "Run fast."

"C'mere, you can't leave," Roy's slurry voice boomed.

They were running on the main road in the opposite direction of the church and Oscar's face appeared in her mind. Her thoughts whirled, but Beatrice realised there was no choice.

"We're going to Mr Talloway. Hold my hand tight," Beatrice stammered over her shoulder, clutching Sadie's hand.

Beatrice's legs ached and her heart grew weary for Sadie, whose huffing and puffing became faster. It didn't matter how fast they ran because Roy's swearing and yelling did not disappear. It was as though he was tantalising them, close enough to breathe down their necks.

"Just a little further, almost there," Beatrice said, panting. Her mouth was dry and wished she'd remembered to pack two containers of water.

Their feet scrambling and scuffling against the street, scrapping on pebbles and debris, Beatrice knew the way to the Talloway house by memory. She didn't need to see the darkened signs on the street posts. After a few twists and turns, Beatrice's body felt lighter as she spotted the familiar black gates.

10
FORGIVENESS

The gate opened and Beatrice shut it with a bang. Gripping Sadie's hand, she raced to the door, balled her hand into a fist and hit the door as hard as she could.

"Daddy's coming," Sadie cried in a fearful voice. "He's... He's here."

The front door opened and Mr Burkes stared at them both in surprise and shock fell across his face at the sight of Roy, his arms flailing around him as he opened the gate and his body swaggering as he yelled obscenities.

"What on..." Oscar said from behind Mr Burkes. Aghast, his brows raised high on his forehead, and said to them, "Get inside, quickly." He stepped aside and the door opened wider.

Beatrice pushed Sadie inside before her and as she fell forward Oscar grabbed her. Someone clutched Beatrice's arm and jerked her inside as the swift feel of air gusted past her arm.

Oscar slammed the door, but Roy kicked at the door forcing it ajar.

"Push, Mr Burkes. Harder," Oscar yelled. Grunting and

groaning, they pressed the weight of their bodies against the front door until the door thumped shut. Roy shrieked with pain and cussed from the other side of the door.

Leaning their backs against the door, Mr Burkes shared a knowing look with Oscar and said, "Now that was a close call."

Gasping for air, Beatrice noticed Oscar staring from her to Sadie, who was red-faced and huffing.

"Some biscuits and juice in the parlour room," Oscar instructed and Mr Burkes nodded. "If he continues to be a problem call the police."

"Yes, sir," Mr Burkes lowered his head and scampered away.

Ignoring the hammering against the door, Oscar led them to the parlour where Sadie collapsed to the floor, her chest heaving.

"Forgive us," Beatrice said, barely able to speak as she choked on her words. "We couldn't stay at home. He left soon after you and we knew he'd return in a foul mood. Sadie was scared he'd hurt me. We were going to the church, but he came back earlier than I thought and was drunk."

"Please, it's alright," Oscar held her hand, it was soft, and he gave a comforting squeeze. "You did the right thing by coming here and don't need to explain. You're both safe here. I'll have some lemonade and water brought for you. Sit and stay calm."

He released Beatrice's hand, and rose from the couch scooped Sadie into his arms and placed her on the two-seater cream couch near the glowing fireplace.

"She's freezing," he said to the servant who placed a tray on the table with the drinks, biscuits and two cups of tea. "Bring blankets and please prepare two guest rooms."

The servant bobbed his head and darted a look of concern at Sadie before leaving the room.

"You were the first person I could think of."

"Unbelievable," Oscar said, and shaking his head, glanced at Sadie with compassion. "It's her birthday, now why did your brother behave like this?"

"He's not a bad person," Beatrice said choosing a glass of water, and took a sip. "He's been down on his luck and it got worse ever since Tilly passed away. We've all tried to help him, but he doesn't seem to see any other way. Tilly is Sadie's mother and died eleven months ago. I don't think he's mourned and accepted her death."

"Yes, it seems that way," Oscar agreed.

Footsteps out of sync approached the parlour. The servant returned with blankets, Mr Burkes declared the vulgar-mouthed rogue to have left and a senior version of Oscar entered with raised brows that dipped into a wedge when he saw them.

"Oscar?" the man said in confusion, his voice was like a deep drum and his thick grey moustache twitched. "Who are they?" His hands were behind his back, gazing down at them through thin-rimmed spectacles.

"Hello Father," Oscar said, hasting to his side. "Let me introduce Miss Beatrice Portly and her niece," he waved his hand over a sleeping peaceful-looking angel. "Miss Sadie. They've travelled far on foot and need a place to stay."

"Hmm, I see," Oscar's father sat on an upright cream couch and reached for a cup of tea. "I see my son's manners have eluded him. I'm Joseph Talloway and it's a delight to meet you." Joseph's moustache broadened as he added, "he speaks of you all the time. You clean our house rather well, thank you, and Oscar speaks highly of your work."

"Thank you, Master Talloway, I'm in your debt. I'm sorry to have imposed on you." She glimpsed at Oscar, whose face had turned a reddish hue. "Oscar has been kind and generous to us both and I think he might have exaggerated about me."

Joseph's laugh echoed in the room and he sipped his tea. "I can see he has not, my dear, the windows and tables have never been polished so thoroughly."

Beatrice scanned the room and a sense of satisfaction warmed her heart at Master Talloway's compliment. She gulped the water and reached for the lemonade.

"I'm sorry; we've run a long way and I'm parched."

"Go ahead, there's plenty more," Joseph said taking another sip of tea. "What brings you here?"

"Thank you," Beatrice said. She'd lost count of how many times she'd thanked them. "I admit it feels strange to sit this way in the same room I cleaned."

Shrieking and yelling in foul language started again on the street waking Sadie in fright.

"Auntie Bea!" Sadie squeaked, sitting upright. "It's Daddy… where are you…? Are you hurt?"

"I'm here, right here." Beatrice jumped to her feet and raced to the chair taking Sadie's hands into hers. Sadie's eyes bore confusion and fear staring at Beatrice. "We're at Oscar's house and we're safe. Daddy can't hurt me or you, I promise."

Leaning backwards, she exhaled a deep breath. "I was scared. I dreamed Daddy hit you."

"No, he didn't," Beatrice brushed away the curly tendrils stuck on Sadie's forehead. She reached out to the table and grasped a glass of lemonade. "Here, drink this, you'll feel better."

Her eyes widened as comprehension swept over her face, scrutinising the room. "Auntie Bea, I know this place. Is this Mr Talloway's house?"

"Yes, it is." Beatrice chuckled and heard soft laughter in the room. She pointed at Joseph and said, "This man is Master

Talloway, Oscar's father. He says we can stay here for the night."

Sadie peeked at him and blushed, giving him a soft smile. "It's good to meet you, Master Talloway, sir."

With an enormous smile, Joseph said with a gleam in his eyes, "The pleasure is all mine, my dear."

Bouts of fury and roars resonated from the street. Oscar called Mr Burkes, who stood near the entrance of the door.

"I think it's necessary to call the police. We can't have Mr Portly shouting in the streets all night. The neighbours will complain."

"Yes, sir, I will do," Mr Burkes said and shuffled out of the room.

"Who is screaming like that?" Joseph said, indicating for one servant to bring more tea."

"Forgive him, please," Beatrice said sitting beside her niece. "It's my brother, Roy, Sadie's father. He's drunk and has obscure views about wealthy people."

"He has quite a profane mouth, doesn't he?" Joseph said. Beatrice noticed the shock on the man's face and didn't blame him.

"Will Daddy go home?" Sadie said as Beatrice laid the child's head on her lap and stroked her hair.

"Yes, he will."

Understanding filled Joseph's face and he added, "The police will help him home. I don't think he'll be able to get back on his own."

Beatrice shot him a thankful look. She couldn't tell Sadie her father could be spending the night in jail until he sobered up.

"What will you do now?" Joseph said appreciative of the pot of tea the servant placed on the table. "You have a difficult decision to make, don't you?"

"Pardon me?" Beatrice stammered as she reached for a china cup filled with steaming tea. "I don't understand."

"What will you decide?" Joseph's cup clinked on the saucer. "I can guess what has happened. Oscar told me it is Sadie's birthday tomorrow. Don't worry; our cook will prepare a delightful feast for her."

Beatrice's head whipped up and shook her head, "Thank you, for helping Sadie, but I'm not sure what you mean?"

"You can't return to your home," Joseph said, stating the obvious and crossing his legs as he leant against the back of the chair.

"Why? What are you talking about?" Beatrice said blinking, and gave him a blank stare.

With a distant look in his eyes, he said, "It hurts the most when the time comes to let go of a loved one. Your brother's behaviour will not stop and this puts you and Sadie's life at risk. You need to think of her well-being."

"I understand, but I don't believe my brother would hurt us."

"Unintentionally, perhaps, but hasn't he already done so?" Joseph cocked a curious brow at Beatrice. "People who have underlying issues tend to take out their frustrations on those they love. They don't want to, they just can't help themselves. I fear that is your brother."

Beatrice glanced at Oscar, who turned away rubbing the back of his neck. She cringed at the memory of him seeing her black eye. Did he share everything with his father?

"It was an accident," Beatrice said, her fingers rolling into her hands. "He didn't mean it. He apologised and said he'd never do it again."

"Yes, I'm sure he was sincere, but let's agree that he has an uncontrollable problem," Joseph said in a kind tone. "He doesn't know how to seek help and for himself, I'm guessing, he feels a man wouldn't need help for anything."

Beatrice nodded. Reluctantly, she had to agree. It did sound like Roy.

"Let me tell you about my wife, Miriam, Oscar's mother, who I believe has shared a little about her. I still love her and always will, but she's made her choice. I couldn't stand by accepting her way of living any longer. It caused both Oscar and me pain and shame. Our friends and acquaintances mocked us behind our backs and we ignored it, despite knowing the truth. I admit that I buried my head in the sand for a while. Eventually, I had to face the truth. The hardest decision I ever made was to leave her, but we are happier for it."

Beatrice's head bobbed and she stared at Sadie's perfect face and ran her fingers over her smooth skin. "Do you hate your wife?" she glanced at Joseph.

"No, I was angry for quite some time. I had to choose to either remain angry or forgive her. I chose the latter," he said, blowing the steam over his teacup. "Though, it was not an easy choice."

Beatrice stared at Oscar, "Do you still hate your mother?"

Oscar shook his head and responded, "Remember our last conversation? I admit I was angry at the time and said many things. As a boy, I did hate her, but then it changed to anger and somewhere I stopped caring. I realised that she didn't care how her actions made me feel. I followed my father's example when I realised why should I hate her and be miserable myself."

"What my son says is right, but forgiveness is another story. Hate and anger come from love and you can't do one without the other. Every day, I'm learning to forgive her, but it doesn't mean everything will become how you remembered or what it used to be."

"Yes, that's true," Beatrice said. "I hope Sadie doesn't hate Roy. He isn't a bad person."

"I can tell you love him, but you must forgive him before you start hating him. I know it's painful, but you are a strong, young lady. I see it in the way that young girl looks at you. She respects and loves you. You can teach her to forgive him."

"Don't get me wrong," Oscar added, pressing his forefinger at his left temple. "I do miss my mother. She was a good mother and her abandoning us hurt more than I can explain. I saw how she hurt my father and with that, I struggled, especially when other children made fun of us. Of course, it made me the brunt of bullying."

"I'm sorry to hear that," Beatrice said. "Roy used to get bullied a lot and protected me when we were kids."

"Bearing a grudge holds no meaning," said Joseph finishing his tea. "But, that's not why we moved here. Oscar and I do not hold a grudge against my wife, but we pity her. One can make a bad decision by holding onto something as dangerous as a grudge. It makes you bitter and twisted inside your heart. If you let it all go, you'll free yourself from the pain."

Beatrice took sight of Oscar's father. Did Roy hold a grudge? If so, then to whom? Could he hate Tilly for dying? Surely, he didn't hold a grudge against Sadie or her.

"I understand," Beatrice said with a watchful nod.

Joseph covered his mouth with a yawn. "I'm sorry, but think I will retire. It's late and I have to rise early tomorrow," he smiled and stood to his feet. "It's been a delight to meet you, Miss Portly. I hope our conversation will help you in some way. Please stay as long as you wish. Both Oscar and I insist you stay as our guests."

"Thank you," Beatrice blushed, her hands grew clammy.

She guessed it might be scandalous to live in her employer's house, but she had no choice. Master Talloway made a good point. It wasn't safe at home anymore.

"If you need anything, remember the rope at the bedside table. If you pull it a bell will ring in the servants' quarters. Ring it if you need help." Oscar stared at her with an intense gaze. "You won't bother anyone, I promise. We employ night staff."

Beatrice gave a nod and swallowed at the thought. It did seem like an inconvenience. She woke up Sadie. "Let's get you to bed. You can sleep in your own room if you wish."

"Mm, uh-uh," Sadie groaned, her voice heightened in panic and wrapped her arms around Beatrice's neck. "I want to sleep next to you."

"Of course, you can," Beatrice said suppressing a giant yawn.

"You needn't worry about your bags," Oscar said. "The servants will bring them. I'll show you to the guest rooms." He paused and Beatrice noticed the shadows beneath his eyes.

"Thank you for everything, Oscar," Beatrice said with a tired smile. Only by sheer will did she not burst into tears.

"You're welcome, anything for you," he whispered with a compassionate and reassuring smile. "Everything will be fine, Beatrice. You're with us now. We'll talk more in the morning."

Oscar closed the door behind her. A dim light flickered from the nightstand. Beatrice walked towards the bed and with one hand pulled down the blankets. She placed Beatrice on the bed and climbed beside her niece covering them with the blankets. Tears slipped down her cheeks and before she knew it, her eyes closed and she forgot about Roy as she drifted to sleep.

11

UNBREAKABLE BONDS

Rubbing her hands over the soft silken sheets, Beatrice felt like she was floating on a cloud. Her eyes fluttered open to the distant birds chirping a harmonious melody. There was an explosion of light filtering into the room through the ornate sash windows draped by lush red pleated curtains.

A lump of heat huddled close beside her. Smiling, Beatrice listened to Sadie's soft breaths. Staring at the room, Beatrice's eyes darted from the drawn curtains to the chest of drawers, a dressing table with a lavish mirror, and a matching chair, which she recalled cleaning numerous times.

Beatrice pressed her head against the sleek pillows thinking of her brother and the commotion he'd caused the night before. Her cheeks grew hot as embarrassment coursed through her veins. Understanding the full weight of her brother's actions, how could she face the Talloways? She'd never forget the kindness Oscar and his father had extended to her and Sadie. If it weren't for them, she and Sadie would be stranded somewhere or worse.

Sadie stirred with a light groan. "Auntie Bea?"

"I'm here," Beatrice said, caressing her hand over Sadie's back. "We're in Oscar's house, do you remember?"

Her mouth opened wide as she yawned and nodded. "It's soft."

"Yes, the bed is lovely," Beatrice said.

"I like it. Can I keep it?"

Laughing, Beatrice shook her head. "No, it would never fit into our home."

Sadie buried her head beneath the blankets. "Then I'll never get off."

"Oh?" Beatrice said, raising a brow. She dug the tips of her fingers into the sides of Sadie's stomach and was rewarded by a screaming giggle.

"No, stop, stop," Sadie's voice squeaked as she laughed. "I'll get... off, I... will, I promise."

Beatrice released Sadie and wiped the tears of mirth gathering in her eyes. "Good, let's get up now. I'm sure it's safe to go home."

Sadie rolled out of bed with a grunt while Beatrice climbed out and walked to the nightstand, pouring water from the pitcher into a large wooden bowl. She lifted a starched white cloth from the surface dipped it inside the bowl and squeezed it tight.

"Come, wipe your face," Beatrice instructed.

While yawning and rubbing her eyes, Sadie stepped toward her aunt grabbed the cloth and began cleaning her face.

Beatrice dipped a second cloth into the bowl and did the same.

After dressing herself and helping Sadie dress into the new clothes Oscar had provided for them, they left the room. Beatrice stared inside the room before closing the door. It was hard to imagine that she cleaned the room. They walked down the passageway towards the staircase and Beatrice ran her fingers along the engraved grooves of the staircase banister. Not a speck of dust.

She tugged on Sadie's hand to follow her to the parlour where she halted in surprise at the sight of Oscar seated on a chair, his one leg crossed over the other, reading a newspaper.

Had he been waiting for them? If so, why would he wait for them? She was just the cleaner of his house, wasn't she? He was being kind to them because that was his nature, or was there something more?

"Good morning," he said with a cheery smile. "I was beginning to think you would sleep all day, but here you are. My father has extended an invitation for you both to join us for breakfast." His smile widened as his intense kind eyes gazed at her. "You cannot decline."

"Are you sure? I mean, you don't mind?" Beatrice flushed, captivated by his optimism and willingness to help them.

"Why would I mind?"

"I... well, I clean your house, and—"

"I didn't wait in the parlour to read the newspaper," he blurted and his cheeks turned a light shade of pink. "Well, I do read the paper, but I've read this one before."

"Oh, I see. If I got a chance to read the paper I would enjoy it, but I don't think I could read the same one again. It would be old news, wouldn't it?"

He stepped a little closer and Beatrice's heart thumped. Willing him to stop, she feared he might hear her heart thump faster.

"I don't mind old news, well, it would be familiar. I tend to prefer what I know to be familiar. Sometimes I don't want anything to change, but rather I want more."

"I-I don't understand," Beatrice said, her skin rippling with a pleasant, but odd sensation.

"Nothing about you is old news," Oscar said, his voice husky and sincere.

"What are we talking about?" Beatrice's stomach twisted into a knot. What was he saying? "Aren't we talking about the newspaper?" she said with a frown wishing the floor would open and swallow her up. When he didn't answer, she said, "After breakfast, I'll read the newspaper if that is what you want."

A grin crept upon Oscar's face, beaming. "Yes, I'd like that. Please, do read the newspaper."

"Oh, yes, I will. And thank you for waiting for us," Beatrice said, glimpsing at him as embarrassment took hold of her. She was at a loss for words and had no idea why.

"Auntie Bea," Sadie said, tugging at her aunt's sleeve. "When are we going to have breakfast?"

"Breakfast, yes, of course," Oscar said flustered. "I mentioned my father suggested you should join us."

Beatrice clutched Sadie's hand, who winced. "Yes, that is kind of your father. We'd love to join you if that's not too much trouble. Then, we'll take our leave."

Sadie wiggled her hand from Beatrice's grip, who side-glanced her niece. Guilt pulled at her heart realising she'd hurt her niece's hand. She returned Oscar's stare and smiled, her heart pounding. Why did he have this effect on her? No other man had ever made her hands feel clammy nor made her feel a rush of heat course through her body.

"Why would you leave? There's no need to take your leave. You are welcome here," Oscar said and then with a frown, "Are you alright? Your face is red. Are you unwell?"

Stammering, Beatrice said, "I'm worried about Roy. Do you know if the police took him down to the station? Did they take him home?"

Oscar breathed a sound of relief. "Oh, is that all it is? Don't worry, let's go to the dining hall, and in the meantime, I'll send Mr Burkes to find out the whereabouts of your brother." He winked at Sadie, "I'm sure your father's fine."

Sadie's face bubbled into a reassuring smile with a nod, and adding to Beatrice's embarrassment, she said, "I'm hungry."

Oscar took Sadie's hand and with Beatrice behind him, led them into the dining hall as if they'd never been inside before.

From the ceiling in the middle of the room, the chandelier glistened cascading like a gentle stream. Mounted on the walls surreal paintings of obscure figures stared as they entered the hall.

"Take a seat," Oscar said, gesturing towards the empty chairs. "I'll have a little chat with Mr Burkes while breakfast is being served. My father should be down soon." Oscar flashed a quick smile before leaving in search of their butler.

Sadie wasted no time and hopped onto a chair to the left at the head of the table as Mr Talloway entered the room. His heels clicked against the floor echoing throughout the room and he greeted them with a warm smile.

"Ah, I'm happy you came to join us for breakfast. It gets tiresome listening to Oscar chatter all the time," he said with a playful laugh and took his seat at the head of the table. "He's spoken a lot about you Miss Portly so naturally I'm curious to learn more about you."

Beatrice blushed as she sat beside Sadie. Oscar returned to the dining hall and sat beside his father. Sadie beamed as he settled opposite her.

The scullery maid, Gertrude Anderson, hurried into the hall with platters of sausages, bacon, toasted bread, fried vegetables and cubes of butter. Beatrice chuckled watching Sadie's eyes scrutinising the platters in awe as the table filled with delicious food. Beatrice had to admit the tantalising aroma drifting from the table was mouth-watering.

"What are you waiting for?" Oscar said glancing between Beatrice and Sadie. "Please help yourself. There's plenty more."

Beatrice and Sadie filled their plates and Oscar appeared pleased as he sipped his tea.

Glancing at her niece wolfing her fourth sausage, Beatrice grinned. The food was heavenly and Beatrice savoured the taste of the crispy bacon dipped in egg and buttered toast. Tasting the tea, she'd never experienced such warm soothing liquid seeping down the back of her throat, refreshing and smooth, its citrus tang balanced with a spicy malt gentle to her palate.

"It's Earl Grey," Mr Talloway said, lifting the teacup to his lips. "Remarkable, isn't it?"

"I've never tasted anything so..." Beatrice said, her voice trailing off unable to find a word to describe the tea.

"Wonderful?" Oscar laughed. "Unlike my father, I prefer a sweeter taste like the English Breakfast tea."

"Can I try some?" Sadie asked, her cheeks puffed out as she chewed.

"Don't talk with your mouth full or you'll choke," Beatrice said.

The door to the dining hall swung open and Mr Burkes strode inside with his hands behind his back and lifting his chin with a solemn expression said, "Sirs, I'm sorry to interrupt your breakfast, but I've received word from the constable and he says Roy Portly escaped police custody last night and his whereabouts are unknown."

The clattering of cutlery falling upon the china plates resonated throughout the room.

"Daddy's gone?" Sadie's voice warbled as her brows shot up.

Clutching Sadie's hand in comfort, Beatrice paled and lost her appetite. What did he mean that Roy's whereabouts was unknown? How could he have escaped police custody?

"What... What do you mean?" Beatrice said, her eyes fixed on the butler. "He's gone?"

"One minute," Oscar said lifting his forefinger into the air. Pushing his chair back, Oscar jumped to his feet and pulled the butler aside. Beatrice inclined her ear, but she could only make out Oscar's questions and Mr Burkes responded in a hushed tone.

"How is this possible...? What else... the constable, what?... Mr Burkes...."

"Oscar, what's going on?" Beatrice said in a heightened tone and her pulse quickened. "Has something happened to Roy?"

"Thank you, Mr Burkes, you're excused."

With a curt not, Mr Burkes left the dining hall.

Oscar turned and glanced between everyone seated at the table with a forlorn expression. "Mr Burkes enquired about your brother at the police station and it appears he has escaped."

"But, how?" Joseph said with a deep frown, staring at his son. "The Captain assured there'd be no further occurrences."

"Apparently, Mr Portly put up a fight and causing a ruckus assaulted a couple of police officers. They were about to transfer him from the police station to prison. He freed himself and ran down the street. It was dark and although a few officers went after him and searched every street," his shoulders lifted dismally, "they could not find him."

"Why weren't we informed?" Joseph demanded, thumping the table with the palm of his hand.

"The Captain had thought they'd have found and detained him by now. He has assured us that Mr Portly will be found and arrested. The police officers have been patrolling this area in the event he returns, which they suspect he might do." He glanced at Beatrice and Sadie with a sigh, "The police suspect that it is inevitable that he will come back considering you both are staying here."

Touching his mouth with a napkin, Mr Talloway exhaled his disapproval and said with a frown, "I agree." He stared at Oscar, whose face was contorted with worry.

"If anyone knows his way around the streets, it's Roy," Beatrice said, recalling the escapades they had as children. "He knows every nook and cranny within the streets. The police won't find him."

Sadie's hand squeezed Beatrice's arm and her face was full of fear.

"I'd like you both to stay another night, stay as long as you need until your brother is apprehended," said Mr Talloway with a stern expression on his face. "You are safe here and most welcome."

"Thank you, Mr Talloway," Beatrice said with a wan smile as she placed her arm around Sadie's shaking body. "We appreciate your kindness."

"I promise, Beatrice," Oscar said, giving his father a grateful nod. "We'll protect you. Nothing will happen while you stay here."

Giving Sadie's hand a quick squeeze, Beatrice said with a comforting smile, "See? Everything will be fine. You'll see. We're safe here. Oscar and Mr Talloway will protect us and the police are looking everywhere."

Sadie returned a sad smile staring at Beatrice with a faraway look in her eyes.

Beatrice toyed with the rest of her breakfast, though Sadie gobbled most of the food on her plate. She suppressed the lump in her throat threatening to expose the tears ready to explode. What happened to her brother? What happened to the young boy who took care of her? He'd been the best big brother, but when did his path change? Was it the death of Tilly? Was Sadie too much of a reminder for him?

Beatrice hoped the police would find him soon and she'd visit him. She'd speak to him so he'd see reason and change his ways. There was good in him. Though misguided, he'd always been a kind soul. Her mind swirled with thoughts of Roy and her determination grew to save her brother from himself.

12
DELUSIONS OF TRUTH

Mr Talloway's kindness knew no bounds. He had arranged coloured pencils and paper for Sadie to draw and had instructed servants to bring some of Felicia's and Oscar's old toys that had been packed away and be given to Sadie to occupy her in the parlour.

"Do you know how to read and write?" he'd asked Sadie as she drew a picture of her home. The fireplace within the open-plan living room.

"Uh-huh," Sadie had answered, her tongue sticking out of her mouth as she concentrated on her drawing. "Auntie Bea taught me when I couldn't go to school anymore. She taught me how to draw, too."

"That's fantastic," Mr Talloway said. "Perhaps we'll find some books for you." He offered a smile and stood to his feet. "Please excuse me. I need to continue with business. I have a meeting this afternoon."

"Thank you," Sadie responded with a toothy smile. "I'll draw you a picture, too."

"Splendid. I need another picture for my study."

Sadie giggled as he left the room.

"Would you like to walk with me in the garden?" Oscar said, facing Beatrice after he placed his teacup and saucer on the table.

"Yes, I'd love to," Beatrice said. Turning to Sadie, she said, "You'll be alright by yourself here?"

"Yes, I'm big now."

"Alright," Beatrice chuckled. Standing to her feet, she allowed Oscar to lead her to the garden that she visited frequently during her breaks whenever she worked at the Talloway house.

Beatrice admired the beautiful colours as she sauntered through the garden with Oscar beside her. The warmth of the sun hugged her skin and she breathed in the fresh fragrant air.

"Thank you for all you've done for me and Sadie," Beatrice said, her clammy hands clutching her skirt. Why did Oscar make her feel awkward, but in a good way? He always filled her gloomy days with sunshine.

"Oh? There's no need to thank me," Oscar responded with a bashful smile. "I only did what any gentleman would do."

Beatrice shook her head. "No, you and your father didn't need to take us in. Other people would never dream of such a thing."

Oscar stopped walking. His body turned towards her and he stared at her. His eyes were brilliant beneath the sun's rays and she swallowed.

"We've endured hardship. My father and I know it well. How could we turn you and Sadie away? It would be cruel."

Beatrice recalled the night they'd shared dinner together and recognised the same solemn look on his face and the way he gazed at her made her heart skip a beat. He cupped his hand over her cheek and warmth filled her. The birds trilled, but it seemed far away.

"You mean a lot more to me than you realise," he said in a whisper. "You're a good person."

He leaned closer, his face inches from hers. Heat flushed through her veins and her breath quickened.

"Mister Talloway." Mr Burkes' voice crooned through the garden.

Instantly, Oscar took a step back, removing his hand and lifted his head as the butler rounded a crown of flowering bushes.

"Ah, there you are," he said with a pleased expression on his face.

Oscar's face mirrored her disappointment as he exhaled.

"Yes, what is it?"

"Your father insists you join him for this afternoon's meeting and is waiting for you."

"I see," Oscar responded in a stern tone. "Forgive me, Beatrice, I need to take my leave. I'll see you later, then?"

Beatrice nodded, covering her disillusionment with a grateful smile. "Yes, and thank you again for everything."

She watched him walk away with Mr Burkes and sighed. What was that a moment ago? Was he going to kiss her? He had been close enough that she could still feel his breath against her skin. Placing her hand over her cheek she questioned whether a future between her and Oscar was possible. She shook her head and removed her hand from her cheek. No, of course not. Why would he be interested in a peasant?

A smile tugged at her lips as she headed towards her room recalling the precious brief time spent with Oscar in the garden. Placing her hand over her heart, she could still feel the touch of his hand on her cheek.

∼

BEATRICE PACED her room rubbing her clammy hands. She tried to sleep, but the moon cast shadows into the room which drew out her panic. She'd climbed in and out of bed multiple times to peek between the curtains and stare at the dark streets. But it was quiet and there were no movements, save for the cloudy sky, teasing her with the moon beams flashing across the cobblestones and hiding the lamp posts.

Despite Oscar's protests, she'd managed to convince him to allow her to continue working. She couldn't let down the families that relied on her to clean their houses. With great reluctance, he'd agreed.

She left the house earlier in case Roy was hiding somewhere and she had a sense of being followed. Whenever she glanced in all directions there was either no one or random workers going about their business.

It was beyond ridiculous. How could she allow Roy to leave her in this state? The sun would rise soon and she was to travel to Piccadilly in a few hours. Yawning, she climbed back into bed and drifted off to sleep.

∼

THERE WAS A NOISE, Beatrice was certain of it, and her eyes flashed open. Shadows flickered within her room and her heart pounded with fear. She heard a thump, then a clatter; she bolted upright grasping her blankets into tight balls. Sweat slid down her neck.

Her ears were ringing, but she didn't imagine it. Glancing at her reflection through the mirror, her eyes widened as Sadie flashed through her mind. Jumping out of bed, she dashed to the door and tried to open it.

It wouldn't open. Why wouldn't the door open? Did someone lock it? Why would anyone lock her bedroom door?

"Sadie," she yelled, except she had no voice. There was no sound. Her voice was gone, yet she screamed.

Pressing her ear against the door, she heard the same clattering and thumping. A shriek filled the air and panic set around Beatrice's heart. Pounding her fists on the door with tears streaming down her face, she continued to scream for Sadie.

Struggling with the doorknob, the door still wouldn't open. She kicked at it, punched it and still pulled with all her strength. Where was Oscar? Mr Burkes? Could they not hear her?

The lock weakened and she pulled harder on the door handle as it creaked open a blinding light filled her room and she fell backwards onto the floor.

Heaving a giant breath of air, Beatrice sat upright in bed, panting. Hot and cold flushes consumed her trembling body. Blinking, she turned to the window and saw the crowning of dawn peeking through a gap in the curtains.

Lying back in a heap of relief, she exhaled in frustration. It was a nightmare. It felt real, too real. Closing her eyes, she steadied her breaths before she slid out of bed and prepared for her day at Piccadilly.

13
SAVING GRACES

Beatrice spent her free time helping Sadie read the books Mr Talloway had given to her. She wanted to practise and impress Mr Talloway with her reading skills and he had shown enthusiasm whenever she read to him in the parlour.

"I'm brave now, aren't I, Auntie Bea? I've slept in my room a full week now," Sadie declared as Beatrice helped dress her for bed.

"Yes, you're the bravest girl I know," Beatrice said, staring at her beaming face. "Well, you are next door to me so if you get scared; you do know you can come to my room."

Sadie shook her head. "No, I'm a big girl and I want to be strong and brave like you."

Exhaling a soft chuckle, Beatrice said, "Alright, let's get you into bed."

Sadie hopped onto the bed and climbed beneath the blankets. Tucking her niece into bed, Beatrice kissed her forehead. Shadows flickering over her pretty face from the dimmed gas lamp on the nightstand.

"Goodnight," Beatrice smiled. "I already think you're brave and strong perhaps more than me."

Giggling Sadie's cheeks turned pink. "Goodnight, Auntie Bea. You don't need to worry, I'll be fine."

Pausing at the doorframe, Beatrice smiled as she glanced at her niece, but her heart imploded like a weakened cabinet full of china cups collapsing to the floor. Often she thought of Tilly and still missed her best friend, just as much as Roy did, and had hoped he would've shared his pain with her.

Entering her room, she stared at the two stunning vivid-coloured paintings of landscapes on the walls. Her heart dropped at the thought of the police finding Roy. They'd lock him up and Sadie would be without a father.

After dressing into her nightgown, she turned off the gas lamp and climbed beneath the blankets relishing in the soft silk sheets and the warm blankets. Her heart ached for her brother even though she knew his actions were wrong. Sadie needed a father to care for and protect her.

Thinking of Sadie, her eyes drooped as she yawned and darkness fell upon her.

∼

"BEATRICE," a voice of urgency shoved her shoulders. "Beatrice!" Her brother roared in her ears and she opened her eyes.

"Roy? What? What is it, Roy?" Beatrice rubbed her eyes and her fuzzy mind began to clear. "What are you doing here? If the Talloways find you—"

"No, they're not," he said in a menacing tone.

Grabbing her arm as he'd done as kids, his nails pinching into her skin, she yelped. "Stop it, you're hurting me..."

"You're hurting me," Sadie's voice gasped. "Let me go. I hate you."

Beatrice stared at the foot of her bed. Roy was in her room? Had he brought in Sadie, too? What was he thinking?

"Come, Beatrice, we've leaving," Roy ordered and grasped Sadie's arm.

"Leave her alone," Beatrice screamed. Removing the blankets she jumped off the bed and toppled over him, landing on the floor with a painful grunt.

"What... Are you mad, Bea?"

"I told you to leave her alone," Beatrice stared at him with a scowl. "You can't come into the Talloway's house and do as you please..." she paused, thinking. "How did you get in here?"

A sly grin appeared across his face and he shot to his feet, his hand flew into the air ready to strike her.

Closing her eyes, she gasped for air, raising her arms to shield her body, but there was nothing.

Beatrice blinked and stared at the same chandelier she woke up to every morning and after every nightmare. Slanting her head back, she glared at the flowery wallpaper as if there was an answer. Sitting upright, her clothes stuck to her body consumed by hot and cold flushes.

Heaving a sigh of defeat, she decided to take a walk in the garden. Everyone would be sleeping and she would not be bothering anyone. She climbed out of bed and slipped a warm nightgown over her nightdress.

Tip-toeing towards the garden, she was careful to not break the silence of the house. The back door was unlocked and she crept into the garden and breathed in the welcoming fresh, flowery scent. Immediately, she felt tranquil and more at ease. Touching the leaves and pressing her nose to the flowers, she deliberated in humour whether to convince Oscar to let her sleep in the garden.

"Fancy you being here," a polite, curious voice startled her.

Covering her mouth to suppress a scream, her eyes widened at the sight of Oscar dressed in his nightgown.

"Oh, I scared you, I'm sorry," he said with a sorrowful frown. "I didn't mean to. I'm usually the only one who comes here at night."

Blushing, Beatrice shook her head. "No, I... I wasn't expecting anyone. I thought I'd be alone." Even dressed in his night clothes, he was dashing.

"You couldn't sleep either?"

"Yes, you got me," Beatrice offered a small smile, her heart pounding. "It's everything with Roy and these nightmares..."

"Nightmares?" he said, raising a brow. "Tell me about them. Come, walk with me. Last time our walk was disrupted, I can assure you it won't happen again."

He swung out his arm and Beatrice giggled, taking his arm. "Yes, lead the way."

She told him about the dreams where Roy was in her room yelling, waking her up. Sometimes having dragged Sadie into her room, ordering her in a drunken state they should escape the wealthy tyranny.

Oscar burst into laughter. "You have quite the imagination, Beatrice Portly. May I suggest you write them down and perhaps in time you'll have a story to print?"

"Hah, don't mock me," Beatrice said with a playful stare. "These dreams are scary. They seem real. It's almost as though it's a warning. But, that can't be possible, can it?"

"Well, I don't know much about dreams or nightmares, but yours are entertaining," he said and stopped. Turning his body towards her, he said, "You can tell me all your nightmares and I promise I won't laugh."

"But, you're laughing now," Beatrice said, narrowing her eyes. "You can't promise what you can't keep."

"Forgive me," he gave a cheery laugh. "It's just when your face is that way under the moonlight it..." he paused, and his cheeks turned pink. "You have an extraordinary face."

"Only under the moonlight?" she said, crossing her arms. "Do I have a funny face?"

Grinning, he shuffled closer placed a hooked forefinger beneath her chin, and said, "No, not at all. Your face is adorable. Especially when you pretend to be angry."

"Pretend?" she stared at him, open-mouthed. "I, well, I didn't think..."

"Don't mind me," he said, planting a kiss on her forehead, and her body flushed. "I think it's time we retire for the night, hmm?"

Her cheeks hot, she stared at him, speechless. Was it her imagination or did he kiss her forehead?

"Yes," she whispered.

Holding out his arm, she took it, and he said, "Now I'll accompany you inside. It would be a shame if you got sick for staying out here in the chill for so long."

It hadn't been that long, had it? Her eyes darted at the sky and noticed it had lightened, but it was the clouds clearing a path for the moonlight.

"Thank you, Oscar," Beatrice said as he closed and locked the back door.

"You're most welcome. I enjoyed your company at midnight," he said, his comforting smile warmed her. "Goodnight," he said with a dip of his head.

"Goodnight," she responded, her heart skipping faster.

She didn't want to leave, not now. But, she was to work in the morning and headed back to her room. Why could she not push Oscar from her mind? She'd always enjoyed the little time they'd spent together, but now she was drawn to him as a moth to the flame.

Smiling, she laid her head on the pillow deciding to try sleeping one more time.

14
RETRIBUTION

Beatrice shot up in bed, her heart thumping in her chest. What was that noise? Did she imagine it? A terrifying shriek shattered the silence of the night and sent shivers down her spine. Was it another nightmare? No, it was real. She pushed the blankets aside and jumped to her feet, ignoring the shocking freeze beneath her feet.

The scream filled her ears, resonating through the air and her stomach twisted into a knot. Exhaling rapid breaths she raced down the stairs. The hallway was clear as she checked every room. Entering the parlour the moonlight shone upon shards of glass scattered across the lush carpet. The bay windows were smashed into jagged fragments soaked by the sweet smell of blood sifting through the room.

Beatrice stared in horror as her eyes followed the dark spotted trail windows, the dark-reddish muck splattered the carpet leading toward the hallway from where she'd come. Panic-stricken, she swivelled on her heels and quickened her steps, two stairs at a time up the staircase towards Sadie's room.

Her heart clenched with dread as the shrieks transformed into frightful cries and she heard the low drum of a male voice. Beatrice swung open the door and gasped, breathless, and her eyes widened.

"Roy?" Beatrice sucked in an emergency supply of air. The room was pungent with the stale smell of malt. Her brother was covered in blood, she guessed from his forceful entry into the parlour. He'd dragged Sadie out of bed, who was sobbing on the floor.

"What are you doing?" Beatrice yelled, stepping forward.

"Get away, Bea," Roy roared with anger and she detected his slurry voice. "My daughter is coming with me! She doesn't belong here." His legs swayed and his feet shifted attempting to maintain his balance.

How had he managed to get through the parlour window and all the way into Sadie's room?

"No, Roy," Beatrice said and forced her way between him and Sadie, pushing him away. "This is wrong. How can you do this to Sadie? Look at her, she's terrified of you. I won't let you take her away."

"She's my daughter, Bea," he bellowed, his feet shifting again. "I'm not going to warn you again... don't care if... you're my sister... I won't—"

Heavy footsteps entered the room and Oscar, with Mr Burkes behind him, grabbed Roy's arms as his arm lifted about to strike Beatrice.

"No," Roy screamed, struggling against the weight of Oscar and Mr Burkes. "You will never have my daughter. Let me go. You... have... no right..."

Beatrice bolted to Sadie's side and pulled her into a tight embrace. The girl's tears saturated Beatrice's sleeves. Sadie's body trembled, her arms clutching Beatrice in a tight grasp, squeezing the breath from her lungs.

"You're safe, Sadie, it's alright," Beatrice said, amongst Roy's yelling and cussing. "Nothing's going to happen to you." She ran her fingers through Sadie's hair, who had buried her head into Beatrice's bosom.

Beatrice's chest closed up with pain, witnessing Roy being forced into a chair. Oscar held him down while Mr Burkes grasped the curtain sashes and used them to tie Roy's hands and feet to the chair.

"Call the police," Oscar ordered, glaring at Roy in fury and Mr Burkes hurried out of the room without a word.

"No, help me..." Roy muttered, his voice softening to a wail. "It can't... be like this..."

"Are you alright?" Oscar said to Beatrice, his eyes fixed on Roy. "Is Sadie alright?"

"Yes, she's fine," Beatrice said. "Well, she will be now. Thank you for coming."

"...my daughter... Bea, you're my sister..." Roy wailed, "I'm... sorry..."

"Get a hold of yourself." Oscar's voice was full of anger. Beatrice had never seen his face full of fury. "This is your daughter frightened at the sight of you. Not to mention you broke into my house!"

"I'm sorry," Roy wept, sniffling. "I didn't mean... Please forgive me." His head lolled to one side and stared at Sadie, who peeked at her father. "I'm sorry," he repeated, tears trickling down his cheeks.

"It's going to take more than a few 'sorries' and tears," Beatrice retorted. "How many times must you get drunk and carry on like a madman? You're better than this Roy. Where is my brother? What happened to the kind soul who took care of me?"

"Stop, Bea," Roy wailed. "I'm sorry, you're right. Sadie... I-I'm a terrible father..."

"Go sit on the bed," Beatrice whispered into Sadie's ear, but she stared at Beatrice with terrified eyes and shook her head. "Hide under the blanket. Your dad can't hurt you or take you anywhere. Not while Oscar and I am here."

"Promise?" Sadie's voice quivered.

"Yes, I need to speak to him."

Reluctantly, Sadie released Beatrice and scurried back into bed hiding beneath the blankets.

Beatrice rose to her feet and strode towards Roy, who stared at her through glazed eyes.

"You going to leave me this way?" His head rolled to his shoulder. "I'm sobering."

"No, you're not sober." Beatrice glared at him with pity and anger. She lifted her arm and pushed her sleeve to her elbow. "Do you remember this?" she said, thrusting a bracelet before his eyes. "You do, don't you?"

Roy's mouth dropped and his eyes grew watery. "You still...?"

"Yes, I still have it and I plan to give it to Sadie when she turns nine like when you gave it to me." Beatrice blinked back tears. "I know you stole it, but it meant a great deal to me. It still does. You mean a great deal to me. I love you. I've missed you all these years."

"You hate me now, don't you?" Roy answered bitterly and under his breath said, "Not that I blame you."

"The police are here," Mr Burkes said, storming into the room. He pointed towards Roy and said, "We've detained Roy Portly. You can arrest him."

Oscar held up his hand and said, "Wait a moment, please. Let Miss Portly finish speaking to her brother."

The two constables didn't appear happy but consented.

"No, I don't hate you and neither does Sadie," Beatrice said. "We're worried about you." She exhaled a long staggered sigh,

"You're a mess and need to get back into shape. Stop drinking. Become a father to Sadie. She needs you."

Roy stared at her and Beatrice saw the pain in his eyes. "I can't bear the pain, Bea. I see her every time I close my eyes and wake to see she's still gone. I miss her."

"I do, too, but you have Sadie... and me."

"You're right," Roy pressed his lips and nodded, adding, "Do you forgive me?"

"Of course, you're my brother. I have every faith that you can get past this. We can do it together, but you need to pay for your crimes."

Oscar gave a nod and the impatient constables untied Roy and took him into custody.

"I'll do better, Bea... please tell Sadie that... I'm sorry," Roy repeated as the constables marched him out of the bedroom, accompanied by Oscar and Mr Burkes.

Beatrice's heart shattered watching the tears fall from Sadie's face, peering over the blankets as the police took her father away. Sitting on the edge of the bed, Beatrice wrapped her arm around Sadie's shoulders.

"Don't worry, you'll see him again. I know it isn't ideal, but we can visit him."

"He's going to prison, isn't he?"

"Yes, but it will only be a few months. It will be the time he needs to heal and stop being a drunk."

Sadie's eyes blinked and squinted as the soft glowing light shone through the window.

"You should sleep," Beatrice said.

"I'm not tired anymore," Sadie answered.

Oscar's steady steps interrupted their conversation and a meek expression fell upon his face. "I'm sorry," he said. "I think I may have behaved abruptly. Perhaps I should've waited before I called the police."

"No," Beatrice said with a slight shake of her head. "You did the right thing. Sadie and I are sad about Roy, but we both feel safe now. Thank you for saving us."

Oscar swallowed and offered a small smile. "Mr Burkes is arranging refreshments in the dining hall. We won't go to the parlour until it's been cleaned," he shot Beatrice a broad smile, "and not by you."

Beatrice chuckled and a smile swept over Sadie's face.

Clearing his throat, Oscar said, "I know now it's most likely the worst possible time, but I can't wait any longer. I've spoken to my father and he approved my request a fair time ago, but I agreed to wait until the time was right."

"Wait for the right time? What do you mean?" Beatrice stared at him in confusion. What was he talking about? Her brother had just been arrested and it was safe for them to go back home.

"You have a compassionate heart, Beatrice and that is a gift. It's the way you care for Sadie, the way you forgave your brother and your selflessness. Not many would go that far, even for family."

Stunned, Beatrice remained silent. Oscar was making no sense at all.

"I've told you I've never met anyone like you and, well, I've become fond of you," he said staring at his feet, his cheeks turned red. "Quite fond of you, in fact, and I'm not saying it right, am I?"

"I don't understand what you're saying, Oscar," Beatrice said with a quizzical frown.

Oscar gazed at her and she held her breath. The intensity of his eyes and solemn expression swept her into another universe. She forgot Sadie was beside her.

"I want you to marry me, Miss Beatrice Portly," he said, lifting his chin with confidence and sinking to one knee. "I don't have a ring right now, but please do me the honour and become my wife."

"I—I..." Beatrice's jaw dropped, her heart exploding in her head. Was he serious?

"That is if you feel the same way as I do," Oscar stammered as if the idea had just occurred to him. "I love you, Beatrice. I hope, no, I pray you feel the same as I do."

"But, what about Sadie?" Beatrice's heart thumped faster than ever and she could barely speak the words. Oscar was serious. He loved *her*, a peasant?

"She can live with us and grow up as a Talloway. She'll attend the finest school and I'll employ a governess. We could buy a house in the countryside and get away from the city. What do you say?"

"Yes, say yes," Sadie's voice chimed in.

"You mean it?" Beatrice blinked repetitively and could hardly believe what he was saying. Surely, she was dreaming.

"Don't make me beg, please, Beatrice marry me," Oscar said. "If you don't feel the same, tell me now."

"I..." Beatrice choked as her heart burst out and tears of joy spilled down her cheeks. "I love you, too, Oscar. Yes, of course, I'll marry you."

Jumping to his feet, Oscar gazed into her eyes with a charming lop-sided smile that grew into a broad smile, crinkling his cheeks. He stepped closer to her and lifted her chin with his forefinger and leaning forward, his soft lips pressed against hers as he kissed her passionately.

Beatrice felt a tug on her robe as Oscar pulled away, his face glowing.

"Does that mean you'll be my uncle now?" Sadie said with a giggle, covering her mouth. "Can I call you Uncle Oscar?"

Oscar burst into laughter and excitement gleamed in his

eyes. "Yes, please do. I'll be your uncle from now on." He hunched down and gave Sadie a tight hug.

Beatrice wiped the tears from her eyes. It was like waking from a dream. From her brother being arrested after breaking into Oscar's house, attempting to take Sadie, now she'd become the fiancé of Mr Oscar Talloway.

"Is this real?" Beatrice said her heart thumping happiness throughout her body.

Kissing her again, Oscar said, "It feels real to me and quite right."

Entwining his hand into hers, Oscar jerked his head towards the door. Though in her nightgown, Sadie was hurrying out the bedroom yelling that she had to tell Mr Talloway that he was going to become her great-uncle and she'd never had one before.

Beatrice and Oscar shared a glance of affection and laughed until the sides of their bellies hurt and hurried after Sadie.

15
EPILOGUE

ONE YEAR LATER

CODDENHAM, SUFFOLK, 1887

Beatrice scanned the colourful seven-acre garden stretching from the woodlands on the left to the right where copse edged the boundary. The trickling of the River Gipping flowing through was a melody to her ears accentuated by the calls of the birds and insects trilling.

The flora was still damp from the night's pattering of rain, a low thrumming against the windows and gabled thatch roof of their cottage. She drew in a deep breath as she ran her hand against her bulging stomach over tiny bubble-like sensations and giggled. The doctor had told her it was the baby kicking and moving around.

Glancing at the noon sun, she was certain Oscar would be back soon from town and Sadie's lessons with the governess, Miss Pritchard, would be over. She never realised how lovely it would be to live in the countryside. It was nothing like the cold streets of London, the airless room she grew up in, in Southwark. The mere idea of the countryside was nothing more than a dream, but here she was living that dream.

Screams and shouts of exuberance drew her attention from the forest concealed by trees and bushy undergrowth. Turning around she saw Sadie jumping into the air trying to avoid the clusters of long grass while running towards her.

"What are you doing?" Beatrice laughed.

Sadie giggled as she almost tumbled over a tiny mound of moist sand hidden within the grass.

"I'll get it right, you'll see."

"What? Jumping over grass?"

"Yes!" she bellowed to the trees. "I've never seen so much grass and trees. I will never stop playing."

"Sadie! Sadie!" Miss Pritchard's soft, but firm voice drifting through the air. "You haven't finished your painting."

"Ah, no... but the rain has stopped. It's a sunny day and I want to play." She stopped and faced her teacher. "Please can we play a bit? I promise I'll finish it tomorrow."

Miss Pritchard lifted a brow as she folded her arms across her chest standing a few feet from the back door. With a lopsided smile and mock sigh, she said, "Alright, but only because you've completed excellent work today."

"Did you hear that?" Sadie turned back to Beatrice and dashed after her. "Miss Pritchard said I did good—"

"Excellent."

"—work. Oops, good, excellent work."

Shaking her head with a wide smile, Miss Pritchard entered the house.

"Auntie Bea, you love coming out here, don't you?"

"Yes, it reminds me of the gardens of the houses I used to clean."

Sadie cocked a brow. "You think those tiny gardens are prettier?"

Laughing from her belly, Beatrice said, "No, of course not. It's like we're living in an enormous park. You should paint everything when Miss Pritchard says you should."

"You think I can?"

"I know you can. Now stop digging your shoes into the sand. They'll end up scruffy and dirty."

"Sorry," Sadie looked up at her aunt with a grin.

Though faint, the clipping sound of carriage wheels touched Beatrice's ears and she stared towards the house.

"I think your uncle Oscar has arrived home."

Sadie's eyes widened. "How do you know?"

"I heard the carriage wheels."

Without another word, Sadie whooped in delight, "Sweets," and dashed back towards the house.

Excitement filled her heart as she sauntered after Sadie. He was sure to have bought more lemons. Since her pregnancy, all she'd wanted was to eat lemons and drink lemonade.

She imagined her as a young girl running around the countryside fields with a younger Tilly. How different would their lives have been if they'd grown up in the country? She pondered over Roy and hoped she'd see him again. He'd written a letter saying he was doing well and would visit, but that was months ago. She had every faith that he'd turn his life around and become the father Sadie needed him to be.

Oscar peered from around the wooden door and stood on the veranda with a handsome smile. Beatrice liked the stubble growing on his chin.

"How is my wife?" he asked, kissing her cheek as she waddled beside him.

"Feeling fatter than a cow," she chortled with a beaming

smile. "Our little boy or girl is active today. Perhaps will be like Sadie."

"You're beautiful," he wrapped his arms around her. "Our life has only begun."

Overwhelmed by joy, Beatrice was speechless and welcomed his soft lips on hers. Never did she imagine her life could turn out this way. That she'd be married to the man of her dreams.

A small hand touched Beatrice's belly, taking her by surprise.

"Oh, Sadie, you're back?"

"Yes, Miss Pritchard said lunch is ready and I wanted to see how my brother or sister..."

"Cousin," Oscar corrected.

"Well, my new best friend is, I mean," Sadie answered with a mouthful of sweets. Squealing, she pulled back her hand. "What is that?"

"The baby is kicking or moving and must be happy to see you," Beatrice said.

"It feels strange."

"Wait until the baby is born," Oscar said, exchanging an affectionate glance with Beatrice. "Then we'll have wailing and kicking."

Beatrice shivered and Oscar pulled her close to his body, which she loved. She'd never felt this close to anyone before.

"Let's go inside, it's becoming chilly," Oscar said, and said, "Before Miss Pritchard drags us inside for lunch."

"Oh, no," Sadie yelled. "She's scary when she's hungry."

Beatrice stared into Oscar's amazing eyes and thought lunch could wait while her husband kissed her.

THE FIRST CHAPTER OF 'THE ORPHAN'S CHRISTMAS HYMN'

BY RACHEL DOWNING

The kitchen of the Winters' cottage glowed with warmth, bathed in the soft golden light of the crackling fireplace. Clara sat at the worn wooden table, her legs swinging beneath her chair, unable to reach the floor. The aroma of fresh-baked bread wafted through the air, its comforting scent wrapping around her like a warm blanket.

"Silent night, holy night," Clara's mother began, her melodious voice filling the cosy space. Clara joined in, her clear, sweet tones blending seamlessly with her mother's.

"All is calm, all is bright," they sang together, their voices rising and falling in perfect harmony.

Clara's father leaned against the kitchen counter, a contented smile playing on his lips as he listened. The firelight danced across his face, highlighting the laughter lines around his eyes.

"Round yon virgin, mother and child," Clara continued, her young voice growing more confident with each verse. Her mother's alto provided a rich foundation for Clara's soprano, the two voices intertwining like strands of silk.

As they sang, Clara's father began to recount a Christmas story from his childhood. His deep, soothing voice wove between the notes of the hymn, creating a tapestry of sound and memory.

"Holy infant, so tender and mild," mother and daughter sang, their eyes meeting in a moment of shared joy.

Clara's father paused his tale, watching his wife and daughter with undisguised pride. "Listen to that," he said softly, shaking his head in wonder. "Our little nightingale, she is. You've certainly inherited your mother's talent, Clara."

Clara beamed at the praise, her cheeks flushing with pleasure. Her mother reached out and squeezed her hand, a warm smile lighting up her face.

"Sleep in heavenly peace," they finished together, their voices fading to a whisper. "Sleep in heavenly peace."

As the last notes of "Silent Night" faded away, Clara's attention was drawn to the window. The world outside had transformed into a winter wonderland. Soft, fluffy snowflakes drifted lazily from the sky, blanketing the ground in a pristine white carpet. The bare branches of the trees were adorned with a delicate frosting, glistening in the pale winter light.

Clara pressed her nose against the cold glass, her breath fogging up the pane. The familiar landscape of their town had been transformed into something magical, like a scene from one of her father's bedtime stories. Even the old oak tree in their yard, usually so imposing, looked soft and inviting under its snowy mantle.

"Clara, love, come away from the window," her mother called, bustling about the kitchen. "We need to get ready for the Christmas Eve service."

Clara reluctantly tore herself away from the enchanting view. She could hear her father outside, his muffled voice carrying through the walls as he prepared the horses for their journey to the church.

"Jane!" her father called from outside. "We'd best be off soon. The horses are ready!"

Clara's mother paused in her hurried preparations, a worried frown creasing her brow. She peered out the window, her eyes scanning the thickening snowfall.

"George," she called back in concern, "are you sure we should go? The weather's turning worse."

Clara watched as her father appeared in the doorway, snow dusting his broad shoulders and clinging to his beard. His cheeks were ruddy from the cold, but his eyes twinkled with reassurance.

"Don't fret, my dear," he said, crossing the room to place a comforting hand on his wife's shoulder. "The church isn't far, and I've seen worse weather than this. We'll be back home before the heavy snow sets in, I promise."

Clara nestled between her mother and the window as they got in the carriage, the warmth of their bodies fought back the chill seeping through the wooden frame. Looking out the window, she could see the snowflakes dance in the lantern light. Her small fingers traced patterns on the glass, leaving ephemeral designs that quickly faded.

"We'll need to stock up on flour," her mother mused, her voice soft and melodic even when discussing mundane matters. "And perhaps some extra candles for the long winter nights."

Clara's father nodded, his strong hands steady on the reins. "Aye, and we mustn't forget a treat or two for our little songbird here," he said, winking at Clara.

A smile bloomed on Clara's face, and she began to hum "God Rest Ye Merry, Gentlemen" under her breath. The familiar tune filled the small space of the carriage, mingling with the gentle creaking of the wheels and the muffled clip-clop of the horses' hooves.

Her mother joined in, harmonising with Clara's melody. Their voices twined together, rising and falling like the snowy hills around them. Joy surged through Clara, her heart swelling with love for her parents and the simple pleasure of singing together.

As they rounded a bend in the road, the church spire came into view, its cross barely visible through the swirling snow. Clara's excitement bubbled over, and she clapped her mitten covered hands together.

"Look, Papa! We're almost there!"

Her father chuckled, the sound rich and warm. "Indeed we are, my love. And not a moment too soon – it seems the snow is picking up."

Clara hardly noticed the thickening snowfall, too caught up in the magic of the evening. The carriage windows were now almost completely frosted over, but she could still make out the warm glow of lanterns from nearby houses. It was as if the whole world had been transformed into a glittering wonderland, just for Christmas Eve.

As they drew closer to the church, the faint strains of an organ could be heard, playing the opening notes of "O Come, All Ye Faithful." Clara's heart leapt with anticipation, and she began to sing along softly, her parents joining in without hesitation.

The carriage was filled with their harmonious voices, a cocoon of warmth and love amidst the winter night. Clara felt safe and cherished, surrounded by her parents and the joyous sounds of Christmas. In that moment, everything was perfect.

Clara's heart leapt into her throat as the horses' frightened whinnies pierced the air. The carriage lurched violently, throwing her against her mother's side. Jane's arm instinctively wrapped around her daughter, holding her close.

"George!" Jane cried out, her voice tight with fear.

Clara felt the carriage tilt precariously, the world outside becoming a dizzying blur of white. The comforting sounds of their hymn was cut off by the terrifying screech of metal against ice and the thunderous pounding of hooves.

"Hold on!" George's voice was strained as he fought to control the panicking horses.

Clara squeezed her eyes shut, burying her face in her mother's coat. She could feel her mother's rapid heartbeat, matching the frantic rhythm of her own.

The carriage slid sideways, and Clara heard her father grunt with effort as he tried to steer them back on course. For a moment, it seemed as though they might regain control. Then came a sickening lurch as the carriage wheels left the road entirely.

There was a deafening crack as they smashed through the wooden barrier at the road's edge. Splinters flew past the windows, and Clara felt herself being thrown forward. Her mother's arms tightened around her, shielding her from the impact.

The world spun wildly, snow and sky blurring together in a dizzying whirl. Clara heard her mother's prayer, barely audible above the chaos: "Lord, protect us."

Then came the jolting impact as the carriage struck something solid. The last thing Clara registered was her father calling out their names, his voice filled with a fear she had never heard before.

**Click here to read the rest of
'The Orphan's Christmas Hymn'**

A Christmas carol. A forbidden friendship. A love that rings true through the years.

In Victorian London, seven-year-old Clara Winters' world shatters when tragedy strikes days before Christmas. Sent to St. Mary's Church Orphanage, she finds her only solace in the hymns that once filled her happy home. When her angelic voice catches the attention of the kind-hearted Reverend Thornton and his musically gifted son Edward, Clara dares to dream of a brighter future.

But fate has other plans. Separated by circumstances

beyond their control, Clara finds herself serving in a wealthy household where her gift for song brings both joy and unwanted attention. Through years of hardship, her faith and music become her refuge, even as memories of her childhood friendship with Edward fade into cherished memories.

Until one snowy Christmas Eve changes everything...

From lamplit orphanage halls to frost-covered London streets, this tale of faith, forgiveness, and the healing power of music will warm your heart like a cherished Christmas carol. Join Clara and Edward as they learn that sometimes life's greatest gifts come wrapped in the most unexpected packages.

'The Orphan's Christmas Hymn'

OUR GIFT TO YOU

AS A WAY TO SAY THANK YOU WE WOULD LOVE TO SEND YOU THIS BEAUTIFUL STORY FREE OF CHARGE.

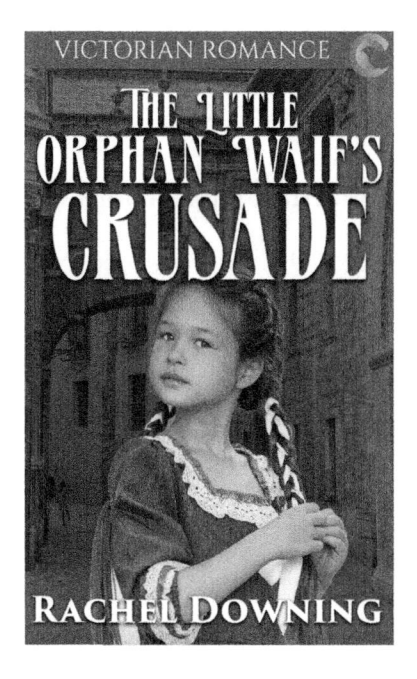

Click here for your FREE COPY of

'The Little Orphan Waif's Crusade'

CornerstoneTales.com/sign-up

In the wake of her father's passing, seven-year-old Matilda is determined to heal her sister Effie's shattered spirit.

Desperate to restore joy to Effie's life, Matilda embarks on a daring quest, aided by the gentle-hearted postman, Philip. Together, they weave a plan to ignite the flame of love in Effie's heart once more.

At Cornerstone Tales we publish books you can trust. Great tales without sex or swearing, but with all of the mystery and romance you expect from a great story.

Be the first to know when we release new books, take part in our fun competitions, and get surprise free books in your inbox by signing up to our free VIP Reader list.

As a thank you you'll receive a copy of 'The Little Orphan Waif's Crusade' by *Rachel Downing* straight away, alongside other gifts.

Click here to sign up for our mailing list, and receive your FREE stories.

CornerstoneTales.com/sign-up

LOVE VICTORIAN ROMANCE?

Another Dorothy Welling's Victorian Romance

The Moral Maid's Unjust Trial

Matilda must fend for herself when her father is wrongfully accused for a crime he didn't commit.

Get 'The Moral Maid's Unjust Trial' Here!

Books by our other Victorian Romance Writer *RACHEL DOWNING*

Two Steadfast Orphan's Dreams

Follow the stories of Isabella and Ada as they overcome all odds and find love.

Get 'Two Steadfast Orphan's Dreams' Here!

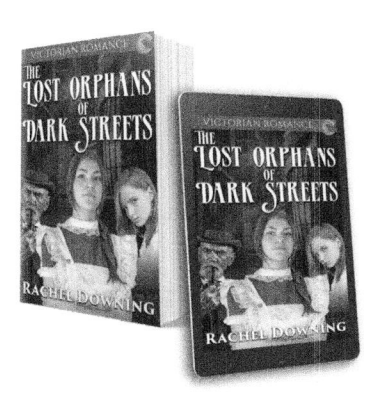

The Lost Orphans of Dark Streets

Follow the stories of Elizabeth and Molly as they negotiate the dangerous slums and find their place in the world.

Get 'The Lost Orphans of Dark Streets' Here!

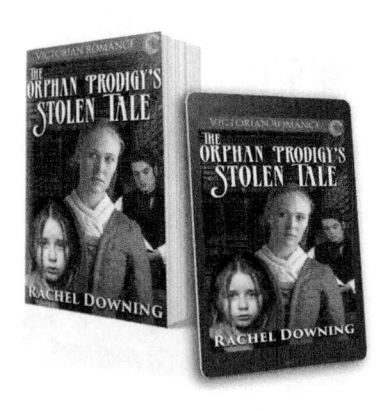

The Orphan Prodigy's Stolen Tale

When ten-year-old Isabella Farmerson's world shatters with the tragic loss of her parents, she's thrust into a life of hardship and uncertainty.

Get 'The Orphan Prodigy's Stolen Tale' Here!

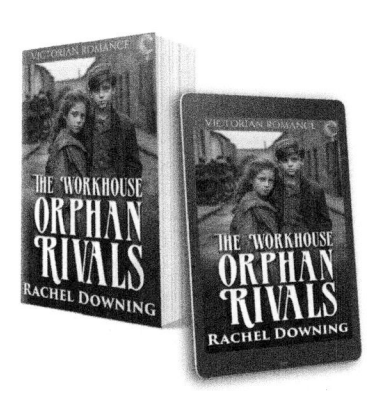

The Workhouse Orphan Rivals

Childhood sweethearts torn apart. A promise broken. A love that refuses to die.

Get 'The Workhouse Orphan Rivals' Here!

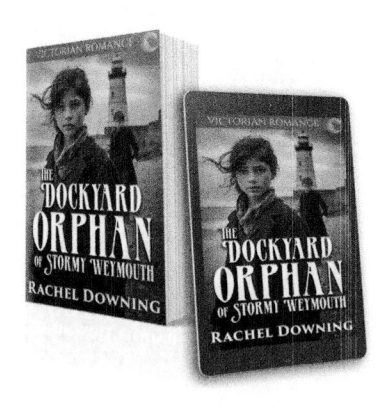

The Dockyard Orphan of Stormy Weymouth

Sarah Campbell's world crumbles when a tragic accident claims her parents' lives. She finds solace in the lighthouse's beam that guides ships to safety. But it's a young fisherman wrestling with his own loss, who truly captures her heart.

Get 'The Dockyard Orphan of Stormy Weymouth' Here!

The Orphan's Christmas Hymn

Seven-year-old Clara Winters' world shatters when tragedy strikes days before Christmas. Sent to St. Mary's Church Orphanage, she finds her only solace in the hymns that once filled her happy home. When her angelic voice catches the attention of the kind-hearted Reverend Thornton and his musically gifted son Edward, Clara dares to dream of a brighter future.

Get 'The Orphan's Christmas Hymn' Here!

If you enjoyed this story, sign up to our mailing list to be the first to hear about our new releases and any sales and deals we have.

We also want to offer you a Victorian Romance novella - 'The Little Orphan Waif's Crusade' - absolutely free!

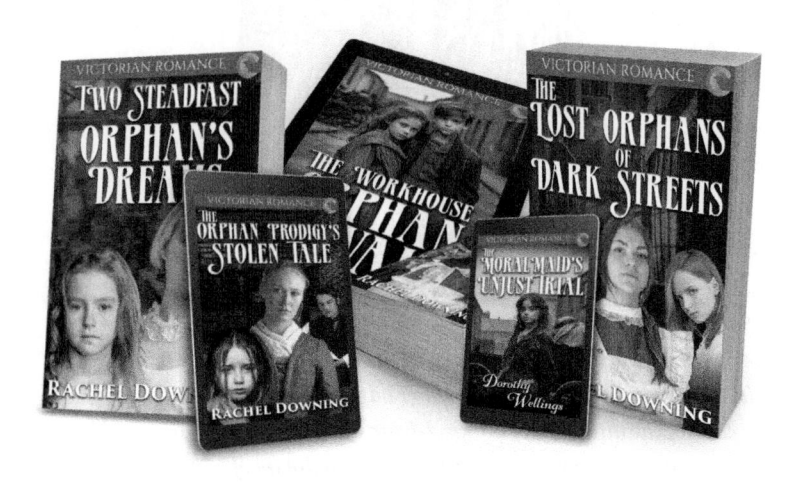

Click here to sign up for our mailing list, and receive your FREE stories.

CornerstoneTales.com/sign-up

Printed in Great Britain
by Amazon